Jake & Emma
Carrero Bonus Book 1
Jake's View

L.T. Marshall

Copyright © 2017 L.T. Marshall
New edition copyright © 2018 L.T. Marshall
Published by Pict Publishing

ISBN: 978 1 7307377 0 1

This book is a work of fiction. Names, characters, places, and incidents are the product of the author's imagination or are used fictitiously. Any resemblance to actual events, locales, or persons, living or dead, is purely coincidental.

All rights reserved. No part of this book may be reproduced or transmitted in any form or by any means, electronic or mechanical, including photocopying, recording, or by any information storage and retrieval system, without the author's permission.

Cover copyright © Pict Publishing/L.T. Marshall
Front cover image copyright © Adobe/Russell Johnson
Back cover image copyright © Adobe/Korionov

The Carrero Series

Jake & Emma
The Carrero Effect ~ The Promotion
The Carrero Influence ~ Redefining Rules
The Carrero Solution ~ Starting Over

Arrick & Sophie
The Carrero Heart ~ Beginning
The Carrero Heart ~ The Journey
The Carrero Heart ~ Happy Ever Afters

Alexi & Camilla
The Carrero Contract ~ Selling Your Soul
The Carrero Contract ~ Amending Agreements

Bonus Books
Jake's View
Arrick's View

Other books by L.T. Marshall

Just Rose

Jake's View

Fans of my books about Jake & Emma will *love* these 'alternative view' chapters.

Requested by fans on Facebook and first shared on my blog as a series of posts, I decided to get *Jake's View* professionally edited so I could put them together in a bonus book.

This bonus book is *not* the full story of Jake & Emma, but excerpts from Jake Carrero's point of view.

The Carrero Effect
The First Meeting
The Holiday: Part 1
The Holiday: Part 2

The Carrero Influence
The Elevator Scene
The Dance

(All are full chapters except for The Elevator Scene)

For my fans.

The Carrero Effect
~ The First Meeting ~

Jacob Carrero stood in his room in front of the large mirror over the vanity and warmed hair wax between his fingers, smirking at the familiar black and gold branded product on the wooden surface. His father was still lording over the decision to start a male grooming line with Jake's face all over the advertising campaign; not that he cared. He was used to being publicly owned, always on show, and every woman's idea of a fantasy male.

Which guy wouldn't? Women falling at your feet every day. Hell yeah.

He rubbed it through his hair expertly and spiked it up toward the center and forward in its trademark style. He was never really one for much fussing over his hair, this kept it sorted and then he never had to care for the rest of the day or mess with it unless he ran his hands through and mussed it up. If he had his way, he would shave it all off, but he had done that in his teens and he had just looked like a menacing street thug and was met with serious glares from Mamma Carrero.

Jake & Emma

He caught sight of the girl in the mirror, trying to catch his eye from the bed. She was lounging sexily and letting the bed sheets slide down her naked body in a bid to lure him back in. Jake just frowned at the effort and went back to getting ready for work. He'd had enough playtime these last two weeks, and she was already boring him. This one was his most recent fuck buddy, long legs, a little too skinny for his liking, and surprisingly plain faced after all that muck was wiped off. Another supermodel who was obsessed with dinner parties where she only consumed lettuce and had her face in his lap at the click of his fingers. Nothing remarkable, boringly predictable and zero conversation in that head. He didn't know why he kept falling into the trap of dating the same types over and over.

"I'm feeling energetic still … if you're game?" She tried for husky-voiced and just irritated him. Sliding his jacket over his crisp shirt and adjusting the cuffs without looking at her once, he continued with the task of getting ready. Jefferson would be waiting with the car now and he had to go. Back to reality and back to running his part of the family empire.

"Nora will feed you, see yourself out." He smirked back at her and felt a tad guilty about the look of sheer disappointment on her face. Just a tad. He stopped caring the second he lifted his shades, slid them on his head, and made his way out of the door.

He was greeted by Nora in the open-plan lounge, wielding a hoover and smiling gracefully, his heart warming a little at the maternal, little widow who kept his apartment for him. He smiled genuinely.

"Can you make sure … Umm."

Fuck, what was her name? Trisha? Tracey? Shit, I've been sleeping with her for almost a week and I still can't remember the damn thing.

Carrero Bonus Book 1 ~ Jake's View

I'm such an asshole.

"Tiffany?" Nora blinked at him and he smiled, feeling more uneasy at his mind blank. He knew it just made him look like a dickhead, and he didn't like Nora thinking that way about him. The woman was like a second mother and her opinion mattered.

"Yeah, her. Could you make sure she gets fed and see that she's taken home?" He smiled again and headed toward the kitchen where he grabbed the coffee she had waiting for him in a steel travel mug. He was running late, and she obviously knew it.

Best housekeeper on Earth, she deserved another raise.

"Arrick?" He turned back to her with a raised eyebrow and then dismissed the question as his brother sauntered from the direction of his guest rooms. "Hurry up, man, I'm already late. Margo will have my guts today, she's all in a tizzy about my new PA." Arrick just yawned and ran a hand casually through his sandy hair carelessly.

His brother was fairer, but had his dad's dark eyes and sallow skin, while Jake had inherited his mother's dark hair and green eyes, and he guessed her looks, seeing as he had been voted New York's hottest bachelor the second year in a row. He never saw the similarity to his brother, but people always said it was there.

"Shut up, I'm hungover from last night. You're lucky I'm even upright, and how the hell do you look so fucking normal?" Arrick was irritable today, last night had been a hell of a party and they had hit the booze a little too hard. Jake was almost immune to hangovers nowadays, years of hitting it hard had given him a more steel constitution than his baby brother. He needed to get him worked up to that now he was almost legal drinking age. He had a reputation to follow and if he was going to keep up with Jake's friends, he better get up to speed with alcohol tolerance.

"You ready to shift?" Jake pushed his brother on the shoulder as he passed him to get him moving faster, he was already restless about being away from work for a couple weeks. He had no idea how much he had missed or what was needed to catch up today. He wasn't so sure anymore that snowboarding and base jumping in between blow out parties had been such a good idea when he had so much coming up. He didn't feel any more rested than when he had taken off with his brother and best mate in tow.

In fact, he maybe should have cut the fun a day early and actually got some real sleep. Last night was a late drunken return and then a lot of sex before his alarm assaulted him way too early. A shower had barely straightened him out.

He shook himself mentally and followed Arrick out through the main door to the corridor where his head of security was waiting with his bag. Mathews looked like a George Clooney of sorts with an air of Jason Statham; the man was scarily efficient. Jake took the bag being held out to him, he wasn't much of a briefcase kind of guy so had a leather messenger bag instead.

"Here you go, sir. All the files arrived last night per your request." He smiled a thanks at the older man and patted his shoulder before taking a mouthful of coffee. A slight stirring of nausea in his stomach at the first non-alcoholic liquid to hit it in forty-eight hours.

Not a good idea at all.

Arrick was practically tripping over his own feet and holding his head. Jake swiped off his shades and propped them on his brother's nose; poor guy would not be any better hitting the New York sunlight in a few minutes, and he felt

Carrero Bonus Book 1 ~ Jake's View

guilty about his suffering.

Jake had goaded him into a drinking competition, knowing only too well he would beat him hands down. The baby boy had to learn to man up with the rest of them if he was going to survive in his circle of friends.

"Thanks." He finally managed after swallowing down probably the worst thing to drink when his guts were fragile. Nora's coffee was enough to put hairs on a man's chest.

Jesus!

With the bag secured over his shoulder, he hauled out the first file and sauntered into the elevator.

"Work already? You have issues," Arrick mumbled from the corner he was slumped into, and Jake could only shake his head at him and smile.

This was the future competition in his father's company? He needed to get Arrick toughened up.

"No. Margo sent this over. My new PA's company record and resume. She wants me up to speed with whoever she is before I meet her today. Apparently, she has high hopes that this is the one I've been looking for."

* * *

Floor sixty-five of the Carrero corporation—Executive house. Lexington Avenue, Mid-town Manhattan.

Walking through the building with a brother who was looking decidedly pale with nausea with his ever-present bodyguard, courtesy of his father, Jake felt that familiar ease move back in. The ease of being back in his own building and in control. This was where he excelled in life. This right here, a building apart from his father's and it was his domain, all business conducted herein was nothing much to do with Giovanni Carrero, just the way he liked it. Jake ran the sports side of the company while Giovanni lorded over the hotels. The grooming line had come to Jake seeing as his face was all over it and he had a million tiny smaller sidelines all being run through Carrero House.

His father had his darker dealings, and sometimes borderline illegal mafia shit, going on and he wanted no part in the old family ties. He'd convinced Arrick to start taking an interest in his side of things; he wanted him working alongside him rather than being pulled into Carrero Tower with the old man. The further he could keep Arrick away from the people his father knew, the better. Besides, Arrick had a good business brain, much like Jake's, and he could be useful in a couple of mergers and acquisitions lined up in the near future.

Jake ignored the constant flow of female swoons and smiles aimed their way, not so big-headed he didn't realize his brother was getting attention now he was getting older. Not that he cared, Arrick would soon find out how boring the female attention could get.

Hell, the guy was obviously a looker, they shared DNA after all.

He stifled a yawn in the elevator and shoulder punched Arrick to wake him up a little, his brother's obvious fatigue was affecting him a little too much, and he needed to look like he was in control. Arrick was still almost slumped in a ball and Jake leaned out and pushed his shades back, slotting them back on top of Arrick's head carelessly.

"Fuck off," his brother mumbled under his breath, and the security guard just glared Jake's way. Jake glared right back, aggression prickling instantly to put him in his place. No paid heavy of his father's was going to try to lord over his relationship with his kid brother. He was sure he could take him, even in here. The guy was about five-foot-eight max

Carrero Bonus Book 1 ~ Jake's View

and looked like he could only bench press half of what Jake did. Besides, Jake had years of cage fighting and mixed martial arts training under his belt, he would give it a go even if the guy was ex-military. With the hot Carrero temper of his, he was sure it wouldn't take much, just another disapproving look his way.

"Get up, dickhead, we're here." He was a little too snippy with Arrick and threw him an apologetic frown, his own hangover was there even if it didn't have the magnitude of Arrick's and he was feeling rougher than normal. He should have had the sense to kill last night's plans, he was sure as hell regretting it now.

Who was he kidding? A night of craziness, lots of booze, a blow job in his car from that feisty red-head, and a night of hot and heavy sex back home with Trisha ... Trudy ... Fuck! Was not something he ever bypassed.

Margo swept out into the foyer in a heavy cloud of Chanel No 9 as soon as the elevator doors opened, like a breath of fresh air, ever-ready with her professional smile and attractive body wrapped in Christian Dior tailoring. She had served him well for years and was the temple of cool and efficient he was looking for in a new assistant. He needed a new Margo to replace her or this was just never going to work in the long run. Previous temporary assistants had either been useless or tried like crazy to fuck him, and he didn't ever cross work with play. He knew what he was looking for and he hoped to hell she was right with this one, he was in no mood for another repeat of Gloria.

That chick had stripped naked in his office and tried to entice him with some oral before being handed her resume and a swift shove out his door. He was maybe a loose sex mad playboy outside of these four walls but inside was a whole other level of play. Jake was serious in business and serious about never crossing that line.

He smiled back at Margo, his right-hand woman and slid her arm in his affectionately, Arrick humphing and trailing behind with asshole, soldier boy in tow. All sorts of grumbles and complaints going on behind them. Arrick was going to be pointless here today, and Jake wondered if sending him home might be a better idea.

"You look particularly suave today, Jake, a little tired though." She smiled at him in that motherly way she used in private moments, fixing his collar over his jacket and tutting at his lack of tie. He rolled his eyes as she shook her head.

"You know they make me feel like I'm being slowly choked." Jake maneuvered her beside him once more and removed her fiddling hand from his lapel. She was being a little too OCD about his appearance this morning, and he wondered if he looked especially rough. He was feeling uncharacteristically so.

"She's lovely, you'll completely adore her. You want your run through as we walk in?" Margo smiled at him adoringly and despite the urge to lay his head on the floor and take a five-minute nap, he nodded instead.

Okay, this crap was seriously starting to catch up on him, maybe he was getting too old for behaving like a rock star. Twenty-eight wasn't that old but today he felt ten years older. God, he needed sleep.

He caught sight of a tawny blonde head over Margo's shoulder, sitting down as they passed the outer desk, a mere glimpse of the replacement as Margo was standing in between them. He was caught by the interesting honey-blonde hair color, anyway; none of that bottled white-blonde crap of all his father's employees. This one looked natural which was rare in this building. In fact, it was rare in his circle. Most girls opted for fakery as soon as they were old

Carrero Bonus Book 1 ~ Jake's View

enough to hold a makeup brush and a padded bra.

He had no idea why that thought hit him as he sauntered through to his own office via Margo's open-plan one, women and their guises were not things he ever pondered. If they looked fuckable, and gave him a hard-on, then that was good enough for him.

PA, remember? No-go ... No fucking.

He mentally shook the thought out of his head and aimed for his desk as soon as they were inside. Margo had been talking nonstop about what he had missed, but he had completely zoned out on her and hadn't heard a thing. He felt irritated at himself suddenly.

Shit. When did he ever do that? What the fuck was he doing? Oh yeah, staring at some chick's fucking hair and having an internal debate on it. Get a grip, Carrero, this hangover is messing with your head.

Arrick slumped into the low couch under the naked lesbian painting done by Hunter's cousin. He wasn't that enamored with it, but the fifty grand he'd paid to give the guy a helping hand meant he had to hang it somewhere. He sure as hell didn't want it at home and no one really ventured in here much except Margo and now this new girl. The New York skyline was getting an unobstructed view of tits and ass, anyway.

His phone vibrated in his inner jacket pocket and he pulled it out, still practically ignoring Margo as she read from a clipboard. All he could hear was "meeting" "lawyers" and something about contracts. This was not him at all and he was starting to realize fighting it was futile, soon as this was done he was closing the door and taking a nap. Arrick looked ready to do the same and he could move the hell over on that couch. Soldier boy could guard the sleeping duo if he had nothing better to do.

"Shall I get her?" Margo blinked his way as he focused on his phone, he waved a hand, and smiled as if to say *sure*.

Let's see what the honey-blonde was like. He sure could use some focus today and meeting his new assistant might be that. He had scoured her file on the way over here and on paper she sounded a little too good to be true. Career girl, smart, no rumors swirling about sexual favors to climb the ranks; young and unattached, so ripe for trips anytime he needed them.

She sounded promising.

"Emma, please come into Mr. Carrero's office. Thank you." Margo was leaning over his desk and pressing the intercom to summon his future number two, meanwhile, he was reading the text from the chick with the elusive name, wondering how the hell he could see the same girl for a week and not have saved her phone number under an actual name. He'd saved it as T.

Fuck's sake, Carrero.

The name Emma swam in his mind's eye and he found himself sounding it out, he liked it. Short and sort of soft, in a way. Easy to remember.

Do you want to see me tonight? I really like being with you xxx T.

"Yes, Mrs. Drake." The voice coming back from the intercom distracted him from replying momentarily; sultry and sort of cute, if he had to describe it and he completely forgot what he was about to respond to T. He definitely had some sort of internal reaction to the sound of her and that wasn't an entirely good thing. Frowning it away, he focused back on his phone and typed out a response, this one had already met the limit of interest, a week quicker than most and the thought of fucking her again did nothing for him all of a sudden.

Look, sweetheart, it's been fun. Let's part as friends and just agree to see each other around. x J

He knew cutting them loose before things got emotional was the best bet and this one had *clingy* written all over her. He didn't do relationships, and he certainly didn't keep the same chick hanging on for weeks on end.

"Ah, Emma, here you are." Margo purred with a voice laced in adoration, this girl obviously had his second in command wrapped around her little finger already, which was unusual for Margo. The woman didn't sway easily. Pushing his phone back into his inner pocket and ignoring the buzz of a reply from T, he inclined his head a little in interest at whoever was obviously winning over his assistant and his body paused.

Black, sexy-as-hell stilettos running up creamy, shapely legs to a tight and figure-hugging skirt, from knee to thigh had him almost dropping his mouth open. She wasn't skinny in that gaunt, supermodel way, she wasn't even that tall, but she had the kind of curves that were made for holding onto and definitely his kind of thing. She was pretty tiny as women went, but that only added to the whole effect. Moving further up past that well fitted and obviously expensive tailored jacket he caught his breath on the most astounding pair of tits he had ever seen. Not overly huge, just soft and inviting and barely concealed under the low-cut jacket and soft silk blouse. Not much on show, but enough to pique his interest. If he was being honest, then a hell of a lot more interest than he had managed to conjure for any girl in a heck of a long time and that was disturbing. If he had met her anywhere else but here, she wouldn't still be dressed right now. A graceful creamy neck that looked seriously touchable and he could imagine holding her around it to push her against a wall and devouring that skin. His eyes swept finally to the face that was turned toward Margo, only a profile but a damned perfect one at that and Jake just couldn't seem to think anymore for a moment.

Fuck.

"Jake, this is Emma Anderson. She's your new assistant in training. Your new number two." Margo smiled his way, and he realized he was staring; she hadn't caught him yet and she sure as hell wouldn't. He wasn't some prepubescent teen with zero skills. Looking down at the floor he could already feel himself instinctively taking calming breaths, regaining composure quickly with all the skill of a seasoned Lothario.

Okay, you're just horny … Obviously! And she's just not your usual type. New and exciting and you have been bored with the likes of women with forgettable names and no tits lately.

"Miss Anderson." Jake got up slowly, tensing his neck from side to side, and extending his hand out toward her politely, trying like hell to not react as that face turned his way. She pretty much floored him with the biggest, softest, blue eyes he'd ever seen. An internal sort of gut-punching reaction he had never experienced in his life and had no idea what to do with. It momentarily stunned him.

She had a soft pouting mouth that could do a lot of damage if put to use in the right way and delicate, almost childlike, features that somehow worked in a mature face. There was very precisely and expertly applied subtle makeup under a sleek updo of soft hair, yet you could still see the girl was pretty. God, he would go as far as saying this one was beautiful, and that was rare coming from him. He had seen and bedded enough models over the years to stop being pulled in by symmetrical features and so-called perfection. She was beautiful in another way entirely, not in a fluffed and preened attractive but a real unapologetic, born to make men want her kind of way. Jake felt suddenly uncomfortable and let his eyes flicker back to that body, hoping to God he wasn't showing just how much she was affecting him.

Her hand felt soft and small in his when she took it to shake, a little too fragile when dwarfed in his and he suddenly got the impression he might hurt her. A tense moment of doubt and he loosened his grip instinctively. Little delicate hands, perfect pastel manicured nails, free from any jewelry. He found himself looking at her hand a little too intensely and let it go abruptly.

What the fuck, Jake? Seriously? Hand fetish now?

"Mr. Car—" That voice distracted him again, drawing attention to that mouth. She had a soft, sultry tone to her voice. Huskiness in the depths yet youthful and girlish.

Fuck.

"Jake! Please." He cut in quickly, to try to get his focus back on track, his brain moving in smoothly from years of self-control and practice to save him from himself. "Margo informs me she's happy with you so far and will be training you a little more extensively in time to step in fully when she retires. I guess that means we should get better acquainted on a first name basis." Jake smiled involuntarily at the hint of knowing her better, his mind immediately dragging her to his desk and most definitely not being allowed to take it any further. He needed to get control of the raging hormones and accept that she was obviously fuckable. He wanted her, she was piquing some primal interest in him and as soon as he accepted that and got over the fact he would never go there, they could move along.

"I'm really grateful for the opportunity." She drew him back in with that voice, and he couldn't help but notice she wasn't reacting to him the way women normally did. He had been too caught up in what she was doing to him to notice and, now he did, it irked him.

What the hell was wrong with him? Why wasn't she flirting and pouting, it was obvious that there was chemistry. He could feel it in the air.

He realized that maybe all that chemistry was possibly one-sided, and irritation hit him hard in the gut. He couldn't even remember the last time he had met such indifference in someone so appealing; maybe Leila when she was like seven, but not any women he'd met since his teen hormones evaporated and he'd filled out and learned to use what God gave him. He needed to get his crap together and just stop whatever this was; he needed a moment to breathe because those baby blue eyes staring into his soul right now were distracting the shit out of him in all kinds of ways.

"Would you like a drink, Emma? You look a little flushed." That tiny pink spot high on each cheek after he had shaken her hand seemed to be more from being uncomfortable about him touching her than any sexual yearnings, and he was feeling really pissed about it. He had no idea why he was being such an asshole about this. Acting like a spoiled, prissy, brat because a girl didn't fall for his charms. Maybe because this was completely fucking new to him.

"Thank you." She smiled a little, a hint of one and he paused for a moment. It wasn't full on, but it suggested that she probably had a pretty smile too, the way her cheeks puffed a little and her eyes softened just slightly from doe-eyed to a little more carefree. It did all kinds of weird crap to his insides, and he had no idea what was going on with him today. He was never drinking that lethal combo of crap he had last night again.

Fuck, he wanted to see her smile properly.

Jake caught sight of Arrick watching him from the corner of his eye, an obvious smirk and that annoying goddamn phone app game he loved to play, blaring away in the corner. He wanted to throw something at his head for the way he was looking highly amused at his expense. No one knew Jake like he did, and he could obviously tell something was off.

Lap it up, princess, it's not often I get knocked off my game and you're never going to get a repeat.

Jake walked to the minibar and found himself mixing up one of Leila's cocktails as he looked down at what he was doing, stupefied for a moment. Literally no idea how getting her a glass of water had turned to this in his head. The only thing he could think was that he was subconsciously trying to impress her, or on some deeper level had decided she simply wasn't a girl you gave water to. She was somehow much classier than ice water. Maybe it had been that heady, fruity, slightly sweet perfume clinging around her that had made him move to start fixing one of Leila's girly combos for her. He literally had no idea what he was doing anymore.

Downing a quick gin to get his head straight, he took back the drink to the awaiting distraction. Margo was regarding him with a really odd expression, probably wondering why the hell he was trying to get his new PA drunk if the clinking of bottles was anything to go by.

Be damned if he had a fucking clue. He was acting all kinds of crazy.

"Here you go." She looked completely lost in thought, and he felt completely out of his depth. He was a guy who had no problems with being in the company of the fairer sex, yet he was acting like an idiot. He decided to perch on his desk, put some distance between them and put all of this down to still being half drunk and crazily horny from last night. He dated women twice her height; confident, boring models, and women with their own money. Women who knew what causal sex and having a good time was all about and he knew how to read women effortlessly—until this one.

She was tightly closed and completely unreadable, no hint of anything at all. No signs of interest, in fact, the complete opposite and her mannerisms and movements were so precisely graceful and swan-like, he felt he was the one being scrutinized for a job. He figured this was the problem right here. She made him uncomfortable because he had no way of knowing how to play her at all. And playing woman in all sorts of games was pretty much his forte.

"Thank you, Mr. … Jake." She looked at him for a second and again he got that stomach jerk reaction he was seriously starting to dislike. He needed to distract himself, maybe stop acting like a complete moron and remember he was her boss. He was versed in the art of conversation, and he just needed to get some sort of professional relationship set in his mind and push this nonsense out. She sipped her drink, and he caught the slight hint of confusion about the fact it was loaded with alcohol. He could only look at the floor, completely nonplussed about that too.

He had nothing.

"So, Emma? Margot tells me you've worked here for just over five years?" His mind gazed back to her file, coming completely clear in his head. He could focus on what he had read and quiz her a little. His photographic memory served some purpose anyway. It was better than undressing her mentally.

"Yes, I've worked on various floors, but mainly tenth." She placed her glass on the table and Jake immediately wondered if she disliked it, if maybe he should fix her something else, and then stopped himself.

Seriously, what the fuck are you doing? This isn't a date in which you need to please her ... She's here to impress you as your next goddamn assistant.

He was seriously starting to get annoyed with himself.

"You were Jack Dawson's assistant for a while?" He frowned trying so hard to focus on what he was meant to be doing, business head being screwed on firmly and the calming of hormones with a seriously stern hand.

"Yes, Mr. Dawson." He watched her forced smile and got the strong impression she hated Dawson but was too polite to say it. He wondered what the guy had done to deserve that kind of dislike and hoped to hell he avoided doing the same thing. Maybe leering at her and thinking about bending her over his desk wasn't exactly going about warming her to him in the right way. If Dawson, the creep, had been openly ogling her then he could pretty much assure he wouldn't be caught doing the same, Dawson was known for making women feel uncomfortable.

He felt a sense of confusion at the irritation thinking of Dawson openly eye raping her gave him. Girls like Emma were classier than the intentions of some sleazy fuck who thought he had a given right to heavy breathe over them.

"It was Miss Keith who recommended you for this position, I believe?" He tried to bring his head back into the game, the sudden urge to find a reason to fire Dawson completely at odds with him today. He was obviously grouchy from lack of sleep and should wrap this up, let her go, and get down on that couch beside his annoyingly watchful brother until noon. He was acting all kinds of crazy in here right now and he was sure some shut-eye would sort him right out.

"Yes. I loved working for her while her own assistant was

Jake & Emma

on leave, she was very easy to attend to and I learned a lot." Jake felt the inability to breathe hit him hard when she smiled unexpectedly, a genuine warmth at the mention of Kay. He had been watching her and waiting without even realizing he was doing it, and it had been worth it. Her whole face lit up, and he had the urge to smile back. He had been wrong about her smile being pretty, it was goddamn mesmerizing. He could watch her smile that way all day and just get lost in how soft it made her whole face, or the way her palest blue eyes turned a hint warmer.

You're being incredibly fucking female right now … Next, you'll be spouting goddamn poetry, Carrero.

"She spoke highly of your efficiency and professionalism. It's rare for Kay to make an internal recommendation for a position like this." Good comeback, he almost patted himself on the back. He had to just pull this off and go to sleep.

"Thank you." He couldn't tear his eyes off the smile that came out at him once more.

"Well, so far I've found her to be a joy. Efficient and capable with a good understanding of the business. Don't think it will take long to get her up to speed with her requirements," Margo said, saving the odd silence with a very weird look thrown his way, even she was picking up on his odd behavior and this was not going well.

Jake suddenly saw the funny side to this whole scenario, being the one panting and getting heated over a woman for a change, instead of vice versa. This is why he was falling to bits. This never happened, and it was completely throwing him off kilter. He was having the tables turned and had most likely met a female version of himself. It explained the indifference she was exuding, he just had to look at her to know men fell at her feet effortlessly, and she was probably as bored of it as he was. They were going to get along just fine if he could notch down the need to screw her a little.

"Glad to hear it. So, Emma? How has it been so far? Learning the ropes of life on the sixty-fifth floor?" He felt better at figuring this out, this weirdness, and suddenly all his good humor was back on form. Relaxing back and feeling more than a little amused at seeing how it felt from the other side for once. Reassured that he wasn't having some weird mental breakdown or had been put under some crazy female spell.

"A breeze." He couldn't help but admire her coolness, and effortless grace. "Nothing I can't handle so far."

"Has Margo warned you about the frequent traveling you might be required to undertake or the unsociable hours we sometimes keep? This job can be really full on, Miss Anderson. It's not for the faint hearted." The thought of spending many an hour locked in hotel suites with her suddenly had him frowning at how hard that might prove to be. He would have to lay off the booze on trips and reel back the charm a little to keep on top of this little debacle.

"Yes, I'm aware that this is not a nine-to-five job, Mr. Carrero. I'm fully committed to my career so it will not be an issue." That defiant little chin lift had him almost instantly snapping back to what she would look like bent over his desk with that skirt pulled up and those shoes ...

Enough!

"You're young ... What about a social life?" He frowned even harder, chastising himself, and giving the inner third degree to that over-sexed, over-creative, mind of his.

"I haven't much interest in many social activities ... I left my home town to come to New York and I don't know many people outside of work." She seemed to hesitate with her answer, a flicker of something he couldn't read. Damn, it annoyed him that he couldn't read her at all. This was probably another part of why he was feeling so frustrated. He was amazing at reading people and second-guessing them. It was one of his most used and highly gifted skills.

But her? She was a complete enigma.

"Career oriented? Can be lonely." He felt stiff and uncomfortable and tried to release the tension in his body by moving his shoulders, his seat on the edge of his desk wasn't as comfy as his laid-back posture suggested and he was barely keeping himself still. Too much nervous energy running riot.

"I'm never lonely, Mr. Carrero … I'm an independent sort of person who doesn't need assurances or company from other people to be happy." He stopped and regarded her answer, momentarily quietened again. He wondered if that meant there was no boyfriend lurking in the background and felt slightly happy at that thought.

"Oh, Emma, that's not the way a young girl like you should live her life," said Margo warmly. "You're so pretty … You should have young men romancing you around New York." Margo leaned out, touching the girl, and Jake could only frown, he didn't like Margo's suggestion at all.

"Sounds like you're trying to talk her out of stealing your job, Margo." He laughed, mostly at himself for his stupid reactions or wherever his goddamn head was. He sure as hell didn't want to be romancing her around New York either. He didn't do romance—ever! He didn't do any sort of long-term thing and knew his capabilities were to fuck and forget. That's why he couldn't go down this route with her, he needed a PA to replace Margo and he needed one now.

Margo was itching to let go of the reins and as she had handpicked this one, it put all question of anything else far out the window. He would just have to get used to the idea that Emma was out of bounds for eternity and maybe he should start looking to small curvy blondish girls to distract him for a while. His body certainly piqued an interest in that direction ever since she'd walked through his door.

"No. Emma knows I value her here. I think she's a perfect fit." Margo turned to Emma, an obvious show of affection on her face that only strengthened Jake's mindset. "Not too sure how much you'll like it once Jake starts running you ragged, mind you." She winked at her and placed a hand on him. Jake knew Margo too well. It was a warning gesture … A Margo special. She'd been reading his body language, knowing Jake was normally far more relaxed than this—she was telling him *no*!

"I'm sure I can handle the demands." Emma lifted that chin again, and he found himself sighing softly in defeat. It was for the best if he just put this chick on the "No-go" list.

"Despite Jake's public playboy reputation, Emma, I'm afraid he's a bit of a workaholic … Surprising I know, but you'll get used to it, you'll certainly rake up enough air miles in the next few months." Margo smiled Jake's way and with a knowing look and a very forceful pat on his arm, he took his visual telling off graciously. Out of bounds, eyes off!

He damn well knows it without your insistence, Margo!

"You'll soon get fed up with seeing the world," he said, but couldn't get that stupid frown off his face, the urge to glare at Margo for reading him a little too well. "And the inside of hotel rooms."

Yeah, hell, he wanted to throw that in there, just for the reaction. See if she was completely immune to being in a bedroom with him, for his own amusement.

"I've seen enough of those to last a lifetime." Margo

waved her hand and gave Jake that raised eyebrow look. He was being told off again, and she wasn't impressed with him right now; it seemed she was also ending this little introduction. "Right, we have work to be getting on with … Emma, you're with me for now." She gestured to the door behind Emma and waved her onward, with one more warning scowl his way, which only got her rewarded with a smirk. The girl smiled back again, only not the beautiful, real one of earlier, more of a relief that it was over, and Jake felt that tug of disappointment that she'd been relieved to be getting away from him.

Definitely out of bounds.

"To our working relationship, Emma," he said half-heartedly, trying to figure out how long it would take to get used to her in this place and stop having a serious dog-humping reaction to her. He hoped it would be sooner rather than later and he was already mentally going through his little black book for a look-alike to quell the frustration.

If he had a look-alike, he was pretty sure she wouldn't be so damn appealing right now.

She turned to the door with Margo to leave and Jake almost groaned out loud, catching himself quickly as his eyes connected with possibly the most perfect ass in a tight gray skirt he had ever seen, his body most definitely reacted this time. The door was swiftly shut after they left, and he exhaled fully, unaware he had been holding his breath for a moment.

That girl was going to be the death of him.

He had always been an ass guy, and she had got the first perfect ten score he had ever given out. Standing up quickly to adjust his trousers, which had gotten too tight all of a sudden, he caught Arrick grinning at him.

"The fuck you smiling at?" he said in an irritated tone, his mind still following that ass out mentally, not impressed with his own stupid display for the last God knows how long she was in here.

"You! Never seen the great Carrero unravel quite so magnificently in the face of a little girl." Arrick got up and wandered to him casually, the same Carrero saunter as his. He shoved his brother's shoulder playfully.

"Fuck off, that was definitely no little girl ... That was a born siren if I ever saw one. Work is about to get a lot fucking harder for me." Jake slumped back down on the desk and pulled over her drink, smiling stupidly at the perfectly shaped mouth her lipstick had imprinted on the side and turned the glass so he could down it from the same spot she had touched.

That's weird, Jake, fucking weird.

"Not my type, but I see the appeal; she's cute ... I'd say marriage material though, so definitely not worth your time." Arrick shrugged nonchalantly at him.

He regarded his brother critically and frowned hard.

How the hell he had got that much from her without barely looking her way once, he would never know. But Arrick did have his skills at reading people too; maybe the foggy lust haze had clouded his temporarily and Arrick seemed completely unaffected.

"Fuck no ... Marriage is definitely not on the table at all." Jake put her glass back down on the table with an arrogant crack of the neck. Pushing all thoughts of that tiny little temptress out of his fuzzy brain.

"I need some goddamn sleep so I can get this head straight, lock the door, the couch is mine and I will fight you for it."

The Carrero Effect

~ The Holiday: Part 1 ~

Jake strolled into his apartment and threw his bag down on the couch. It had been a long trip and an even longer week, but he suddenly felt restless at being back. Normally, getting home brought him all kinds of joy, but this time it felt slightly empty, and he actually wished they'd stayed at that damn dance just so he could still be with her right now. Pacing to the window and looking out across the New York skyline he ran his hand through his hair and cracked his neck in a bid to release some of the tension building up his spine. Flexing his arms over his head and straining the jacket holding him tight. He needed to get out of this monkey suit they called a tux and get comfy, maybe he just needed to feel less business-like and properly relax. Maybe he needed a drink.

He needed to stop fixating on Emma; it wasn't healthy, and the constant stream of thoughts he had about her was getting harder to control. She had been too alluring tonight, that dress had driven him crazy and dancing up close no longer felt safe anymore. He'd made them leave for her sake as much as his own. It was getting to the point he could no longer trust himself not to try kissing her again whenever he was drunk. He wished he had a memory of Chicago, the night she said they had kissed. He wanted to know what it felt like to kiss that sexy pouted mouth fully. Not just a second of brushed lips but a real, deep and meaningful, kiss. He already knew that was an awful idea, she had this much of an effect on him now, a kiss would seal his fate.

Picking up the remote from his coffee table he hit the stereo control and his iTunes playlist came to life, and he turned it up to consume the entire apartment before he headed for his shower; peeling off the bow tie and jacket as he walked into his room. Smiling as lyrics from a song Emma had sent him followed through and he couldn't help thinking of those blue eyes and quick smile and feeling a hint of longing to have her here right now.

God, he missed her already.

The thought hit him in the stomach and he tried to ignore it. They had literally separated less than an hour ago to come home and he was being unbelievably pathetic. He knew he was becoming too attached to her in ways that would make working impossible; always wanting her around and it bothered him because he could tell she didn't feel the same way. He had tried to convince himself a million times that it was because they were more than work colleagues, they were friends. Real friends, maybe even best friends. He was pretty sure he told her more than anyone he knew and that counted for something. He needed to realize what they had was already special. She was too special to him to fuck this up with sex or one-sided emotions.

That first kiss in the hotel had thrown him, had started all of this. He didn't fully understand all the feelings related to it at the time but he sure as hell knew that it wasn't as platonic as he tried to tell himself.

Emma had been shocked, non-responsive, and scared even, and as shit as it made him feel, he couldn't get the feel of her mouth out of his head. For a moment, he had kissed her, and it felt like nothing he had ever known before. His stomach had tingled, his heart rate accelerated, and he had just become zoned-in on everything about her as though time had stood still. He had imprinted every single detail of that night to memory. Her smell, her hair, the way she felt, that goddamn nightdress that plagued him and how it clung to her perfect body. Underneath all her tailored suits and precise clothing was a body made for seduction and she had him with one look.

Since then things had only got worse, every touch, every look, every smile, only served to torture him. It was long past sex, even he could admit that to himself. Right now, just having a chance at another night wrapped up together in a bed would be enough. He never wanted to forget what sleeping beside her had felt like; he had done something he never did with a woman. He had wrapped her in his arms and kept her close all night, unable to set her free even if she wanted to. He had thought that fucker Vanquis had been the cause, but that was a lie. He would always hold her that way given the opportunity. She brought something out of him that he couldn't explain, a need to shield her and keep her close.

He tried to shake her out of his head; something he was getting good at since employing her, but tonight she wouldn't budge. He was falling hard, and he had no way to stop it. Emma was everything he needed, and he hadn't even seen it coming. That perfect, angelic face and soft voice, the tiny, perfect body that made him want to protect her always. Everything he learned about her as time went by made him all the more fiercely protective of her. She wasn't the girl she showed the world; she was so much more. A vulnerable, beautiful, perfection that men had tried to destroy, men he would kill with his bare hands given half a chance and wouldn't regret doing it. She was strong in a quiet, gentle way but she was also vulnerable and made him feel a hundred feet tall.

He could still smell her perfume on his shirt from dancing with her tonight and still feel the way her body molded to his effortlessly. Looking down, he realized he still hadn't pulled any of his clothes off despite turning the shower on. Suddenly unwilling to be parted from the smell of her.

Get a grip, man, you need to stop this shit.

He stalked back to his bedroom from the en suite and sat down on the bed, his hand automatically swiping his phone out before his brain connected the dots. He wanted to talk to her, despite only just leaving her, he needed to reach out. Maybe if he did, then this feeling would shift, and he could go back to enjoying time home. Go back to trying to accept that this was never going to happen and actually get his life back. He hated how little control he had anymore, how much she had changed him, and how much he had let her.

He didn't even drink or party as much anymore. Each time he got drunk he would call her with some lame ass excuse for drunkenly waking her at stupid o'clock. Even before he knew what was happening to him, his drunk self had always wanted to speak to her at the most inappropriate times. He had calmed down so much of his lifestyle, just so he could be around her more, work more, no hangovers invading time spent around her. A part of him wanted to show her he was capable of being so much more than the

Jake & Emma

reputation that hung over him. He liked being around her way more than he liked hanging out in a nightclub with Daniel nowadays.

Jake Carrero, playboy billionaire heart breaker was fast losing that title.

What are you doing? He texted her before sense stopped him.

He rubbed his face and once again tried to evaluate what the hell he was doing. He had tried to play off the lack of dates tonight, but the truth was he didn't want to see anyone else right now. Women had stopped appealing to him the more he got to know her, and casual sex had lost its sparkle. He got more from spending a day with her at work than hours fucking some pointless girl, and it was messing his head up badly. He should go out, get drunk with Danny, and fuck someone. Get rid of all this tension building up in him, he knew a lot of it was the lack of sex.

Staring at a sea of pointless clothes and wondering how I'm going to wrestle Donna's gold card away from those itchy fingers.

She replied quickly, a smile hitting him as soon as he saw her name on screen and that goofy sense of elation that made him snarl at himself. He sighed and frowned at the phone. All thoughts of sex with someone else dispersing.

Jesus, he had no handle on this at all.

Can I come stare with you?

He sent it before thinking and then cursed himself out for it. He was acting like some desperate teen with a crush. Breaking every rule known to mankind on the etiquette of "platonic" friendships but he just wanted to be back with her.

Jake, back off … Leave her be.

What's the matter, Mr. Carrero? Are you lonely in your ivory tower without me?

Her face swam in his mind's eye, that sexy little smile she gave when she was being playful. The innocent flirting, she probably wasn't even aware she did, in fact, he guaranteed she didn't. To her, he was just Jake, good old boss and friend, and everything between them was light-hearted and fun. Every warning alarm in his brain was going off, telling him that for his own sanity he needed to just leave well alone, but his fingers were replying without any permission from him.

Maybe.

He could hardly admit that he was missing her crazily, pining like some love-sick fool over being apart for an hour. He knew he should be putting down the phone, turning it off, and heading straight out that door to the nearest bar with any of the guys he hung out with. He should be concentrating on finding a woman. Fuck it—twins, and fucking Emma out of his head.

If you're that bored, how can I deny you my sparkling company?

Fuck.

Walk away, Jake, stop!

He knew this was stupid, working beside her was one thing, sharing hotels borderline, but actually going to hers socially after hours like this? Completely fucking stupid. He was blurring the lines of what they were more and more, the holiday idea was even more stupid but part of him couldn't let it go. He wanted to see her have fun, kick back with him around to look after her. He wanted to take her away, to the boat, to sun and sea, and he had to admit the thought of seeing her in a bikini had his blood pulsing.

Are you home alone?

If others were home, then it would be better, not just the two of them. He had never been into her apartment before, couldn't believe he was even considering it, but he was sure they would be in a smaller space than a hotel suite and most likely near her bed. He was trying so hard to tell himself that this is what friends did—hung out after work—but he already knew it was a lame excuse. He wanted her.

Aren't I always?

Fuck.

I'll be there in 20 minutes.

Why, Jake, why?

He stared at his own reply for a moment and sighed. His mind and body always at war with how he was supposed to treat her nowadays. How could he be rational when his own head was acting like an idiot and throwing caution to the wind? He ran his hands through his hair, dropping his head between his knees and scratching his scalp slowly. He rolled his shoulders and tried to rationalize.

His feet pulled him to his wardrobe while his head was still telling him to cancel, not just this but the boat trip. Emma had never shown any hint of wanting more, not even a onetime fling. He wouldn't have done it even if she had. The one-night thing that was, he would happily give her more even if it scared him shitless. She was a girl you gave it all to, nothing less, and one night would never be enough for him.

* * *

He floored the pedal to the metal as he hit Queens, getting closer to her apartment made him impatient and his car liked being opened up on the straights. The thrill of a car with this much power meant it demanded a little release every so often. He loved his car almost as much as he loved the girl he was driving toward.

Wait! What? Fuck … Did he just think that? Love?

Getting to the apartment he remembered from bringing her here a year ago, he raced up the internal stairs two at a time, heart a little erratic still, from the adrenaline of flooring his sports car and getting here in record time. Trying not to think too hard about the love thing, he just pushed it back down. It was dumb and impulsive, and he hadn't really thought about that whole love thing; sure, he knew he had feelings for her, but love? He had no goddamn clue. He couldn't love Emma, she had never asked that of him and he had been pretty sure he was incapable of feeling that way, given the number of women who had tried to get it from him.

The asshole boyfriend of her roommate let him in after a quick knock on the door and he couldn't help himself glaring a little. He knew Emma didn't rate him highly for whatever reason and that was enough reason for him to dislike him too. He didn't say much, just a shrug and nodded toward a room down the hall which he assumed was Emma's, they both sort of grunted instead of conversed. Returning to caveman behavior was fine with him; if this asshole ever laid a finger on his girl he would happily caveman-style smash his skull in.

Jake walked past him, towering over him by a few inches in height and most definitely out-muscling him. Jake was already sizing him up in his head for possible outcomes if he ever needed to get heavy-handed on this one; heading toward Emma's room and keeping an eye on the retreating idiot.

The door was sitting open, all thoughts of her pushing away the asshole, and he slid into the space. Instantly assaulted by her enticing perfume and the girlishness of her bedroom. It was like suddenly stepping into Emma's head, a secret part of her, and he couldn't help but look around, a little overwhelmed.

All soft grays and silvers, a cozy stylish boudoir of sorts, cuddly bears on the bed and a million cushions. Pictures on the wall of scenery, mainly New York skyline and some more tranquil black and white stills. The room had a matureness to it, but the small soft touches, candles, trinkets, and sparkly things hinted at a girly-girl that she kept hidden from view. Jake felt like he was intruding suddenly, it was like seeing a part of her that even he hadn't seen. The romance book on the night stand surprised him.

"Hey." He smiled and threw a thumb over his shoulder, indicating asshole's presence; he wanted to know if he had bothered her. She shook her head, but he could tell she wasn't relaxed and it made him frown. If that dickhead had done or said anything he would literally kill him. Her face softening and that pretty smile calmed his aggression almost immediately, his eyes slid to the floor at the Everest of girls' things in a bid to avoid the way he wanted to stare at her mouth. He had never really got control of the staring thing when it came to her face, he had to stop himself doing it a hundred times a day.

"You weren't wrong … I think Donna has dressed you for a year." He tried to turn his attention anywhere but Emma in jeans and a T-shirt. She looked like a college student and cuter than hell. He had seen her in various casual attire on long trips but being here, surrounded by her things, made it different somehow. Like she was letting him in on her completely unguarded and relaxed, seeing her in a new setting. She didn't even seem to find it weird that he was here at all, another hint at the fact she thought all of this was harmless. Friends—that's all she saw in this and that was a sobering thought.

He sat down on the floor in front of the huge mountain of clothes a little guiltily. Jake sighed under his breath.

He knew this, and he had to stop ignoring it.

"Whose fault is that? Mr. Oh, buy her an outfit for this, that, and the next thing, every time you see her." Emma poked him playfully in the ribs and he curbed the urge to grab her hand and haul her into his lap. Lately, his hands-on approach was becoming a little too hands-on. He had practically molested her out jogging in Seattle, too much of a pull to always touch her. He leaned back in a bid to stop himself from initiating playful pushes, she brought it out in him, just by being near.

"Maybe I should tell her to ask you when you need something from now on." He held his hands up, trying to appear apologetic but Emma didn't need to know how many times a week he sent Donna pictures of dresses or clothes or even requests and told her Emma needed them. He had no idea what that was all about; women's fashion didn't interest him, but seeing Emma wearing expensive clothes made him happy. He didn't care if she never wore half of them, he just liked making sure she always had what she needed, and she always looked too beautiful for words. It was worth abusing the company credit accounts.

"That would be an idea," Emma smirked, and he couldn't help but smile back, he loved when she tried to sass him. The girl who had once been so closed off and reserved had come out of her shell in the past few months, he had loved watching her bloom. He liked this version of her a lot more than the closed-off ice maiden of those first few weeks.

"Get rid of what you don't want." He shrugged; he didn't care if she threw what she didn't like away, it was only

Jake & Emma

money. He pulled a pale-pink dress from the pile that caught his interest and held it up to admire it but something else caught his eye before he really examined it.

Lingerie. Much more interesting.

He leaned in for it and winked Emma's way cheekily, damn sure he was getting an eyeful of that baby. He held up a corset type thing, all lace and structure, and really wanted to not be picturing it on her right now, but his mind was making a good go of it. She whipped it out of his hands almost immediately and threw it off behind him toward a tall glass set of drawers with a hint of a blush. Not that he minded; his thoughts had definitely gone down the gutter, and that wasn't a good thing.

"Most of it still has tags, Jake, she should return them." She sounded childlike and almost hopeless. Lifting clothes up in frustration at him. Jake raised an eyebrow her way at the cuteness of that statement. The money he had Donna spend on clothes for Emma was nothing in the grand scheme of things.

"Just give them away, Emma, they're already paid for." He shrugged nonchalantly, sometimes he forgot that she didn't come from his world. She fitted in so effortlessly, so graceful, and never balked around grandeur. She really was fucking perfect.

"Jake, there's thousands of dollars' worth of stuff here." She sounded frustrated with him, but it only made him smile. She had no idea how cute she could be; one second all seductive and irresistible and the next childish and endearingly sweet, so much so it gave him the urge to squish her. Adorable was the only word he could conjure up for her sometimes. He had never been one to think any girl was that, but Emma sure was.

"And?" He just shrugged, he honestly didn't care. It was just money.

"So, I should just donate it? … What I don't need?" She asked sardonically, eyeing him up in her haughty PA way. She tried this look on him a hundred times a day, but it had zero effect. He found it entertaining that she could close down anyone in the building with a glare, yet to him, it was just amusingly cute as fuck.

"They're your clothes, *mio amore.*" He shifted on the floor picking up another dress, this time having a closer look at it and looking at her as he tried to picture her in it. She threw him a disdainful look and started throwing items to the door for donating, a look on her face that almost said it was painful for her. Emma would need to get used to money if she was going to stick with him, he had no intention of seeing her live a life without it, even if she never saw him as anything more than a friend. He would always take care of her.

"You've never worn this?" He raised an eyebrow at her questioningly. It was pretty; somehow her. He wanted to see her wear it; red and floaty and short. Not too clingy yet romantic and something he had never seen her try.

"Nope." Blunt and to the point, she barely looked its way, but he was determined now. She would look good in red, she had the fair hair and porcelain skin to pull it off. Her blue eyes would make it perfection.

"Why not? It's nice, kind of cute, but sexy." He held it up to get a better idea of the style and really tried to picture her in it.

"Where would I wear it?" She smiled his way a little unsure.

"Take it with us on our trip. Parade around on deck for

me in it." He put the dress on the bed to make sure it got kept with the clothes she was keeping, he wanted to see her in it more than anything. He wanted to see Emma dressed all girly and floaty and carefree. More than he wanted to see her in her underwear, which completely confused him.

Was Carrero losing his edge? Libido wavering? Turning into a fucking woman?

"Just the two of us?" she asked him nervously and it distracted him, he couldn't help but feel the sunken weight at how nervous she seemed to be with that thought.

"Not if that makes you uncomfortable … I have friends we could invite; my father's boat has six double cabins if you want a crowd." He tried to focus on the clothes on the floor rather than let her see that it disappointed him—he wanted her alone. Just the two of them, but he knew how disastrous that would be.

"Who would you invite?" She looked his way with a furrowed brow, cuteness personified, and he had to fight the urge to smooth it out with his thumb.

"Daniel, a couple of the guys I sometimes take trips with, and whoever they want with them … I was thinking Leila Huntsberger, that way you could meet Sophie's new sister." He tried for nonchalant and seemed to pull it off, picking names right from the top of his head. Leila would like her, he could see them gelling and that made him happy. He wanted his friends to like her. Daniel had finally stopped leering her way whenever they crossed paths after more than a dozen death threats from him.

"So, they're going to be couples?" She looked scared suddenly and that familiar gut kick hit him.

Fuck. Always a reminder of what they would never be.

"Really, Emma?" He sighed in irritation at the reality of

this situation, annoyed and being an asshole. She hadn't done anything wrong. "What do you think I'm going to do? Try to seduce my PA because we're surrounded by couples and I'm incapable of abstaining from sex? I may always be trying to chat you up but I'm not an idiot. I know where the boundaries are, *bambino.*"

Yeah, sure he did … He just chose to fucking forget them frequently. Asshole.

"No, it's just … it will be awkward." She looked at the clothes and started pulling through them, obviously avoiding his eye. He sighed at making her feel this way. Softening his tone and trying to stop being a dickhead.

"Why?" he said softly.

"They might think we're …" She hesitated and caught his eye. Jake tried to relax back and look completely blank. More than anything in the world he wanted her trust, but that spike of irritation still lingered inside of him though, peeking out.

"Who cares what they think? I don't give a shit what anyone thinks, Emma … I need a break and so do you. Stop overthinking and just agree. Besides, they're my friends, they'll know right away that we're not screwing." He slid his hands behind his head, frowning at his own snarkiness and tried to shrug it off. It wasn't fair on her, his little mood swings because of his feelings for her. She never asked him to get hung up on her, and she sure as hell hadn't encouraged it in any way. He needed to stop and take a step back. Be friends, because if that's all she was offering then he wanted it. It was better than not knowing her at all. Life without Emma wasn't a life worth knowing.

"Okay, for God's sake." She put her hands up in defeat, then looked shyly his way with the hint of a smile. "Don't laugh, Jake, but I don't own anything I could wear on a beach or a boat."

He couldn't help but smile back at her, at the irony.

She really was beautiful.

* * *

Jake had pulled out all the stops to get the trip together in record time; once he had the idea in his head and knew she wanted it to happen he was all over it. A few calls here and there and a few nudges and everything was set. He had steam- rolled over her doubts, refusing to let her back down, and they had got there without any more arguments. His mind was set to seeing her in a bikini, not that he would be able to do anything about it, but still. It was a sight he wasn't passing up. That tense ache in his groin had only reminded him how badly he needed sex lately. He wasn't a guy who had ever gone extended periods without and now here he was, starting to doubt his ability to relax. She would be walking around semi-naked and he was almost spring loaded like this.

Fuck, he should have gone out in a glory of drink and fucking before this trip.

* * *

She seemed completely in awe of his dad's cruiser. Jake had seen it a million times, so to him, it was nothing special. A long yacht, white like every other and sat in an idyllic port surrounded by blue sea and white sands. Just being surrounded by sun, friends, and her was enough to lift his mood tenfold. If he could push the lustful thoughts aside,

Carrero Bonus Book 1 ~ Jake's View

they could have a really good time here.

The crew was under orders to keep out of the way; he didn't want her feeling intimidated by them. He knew she wasn't someone who liked wealth being a showy thing, and he was damned if he was going to make her uncomfortable with anything while here. She had been forewarned that he was taking care of anything and everything, including shopping trips if she wanted them. He had felt like an ass as she had blinked at him, aching to argue but in this, his word was final. Date or not, he was old-fashioned, he paid for his girl. Even if he wasn't sleeping with her.

His friends had all been forewarned to behave; no jokes about being his secretary or any of the men trying their luck. He would literally beat them to death with their own shoes if they tried. He hadn't exactly been happy to see Marissa in tow with Vincent. He had no idea what her fucking game was being on this boat, but he sure as hell wasn't being drawn into any little Marissa games. Vincent was an idiot, he should have known she would sucker one of the twins, they'd always trawled along after her in hopes of a date.

He hadn't seen her since the night he had stupidly got drunk and fucked her, not that he could remember. He had no clue how he had even ended up with her that night, he must have been royally messed up and if she thought there would ever be a repeat, she was wrong. He would throw her overboard if she got in his way. He was happy to ignore her presence, knowing it would annoy her more than having her escorted off. Emma need never know anything about her or who she ever was to him. It was history and nothing he would ever rehash.

Daniel was keeping his distance, just like Jake had told him to. Emma wasn't one of his playthings, and he knew better than to cross Jake.

Jake & Emma

There were six of them with Jake and Emma on the boat, he figured a crowd would give him more chance to get time alone with her than just another couple of people. With them were Daniel in all his tanned blond glory and the twins, Vincent and Richard, white-blond hair and gray eyes, all American good looks and square shoulders on all three.

Leila was wandering about on deck having some sort of bitchy glaring competition with Marissa and Miracle, Daniel's porn star, and this was the last thing he needed. At least Leila wasn't being viperous to Hunter for once. Seemed things had finally cooled down with them after months of frosty glares. Being in the same place again without toxic warfare was pretty great. He would have to warn her about starting anything with either girl, not that he worried Leila couldn't handle them, the exact opposite in fact. If Leila flew off the handle, it would be an airlift to the coast ER for two females and Leila wouldn't be one. He had bad memories of Leila taking on some of Daniel's dates in the past and flying bottles.

Jake had already had to deflect advances from the leggy porn star who, while topless, had tried to grapple him alone in the lower hall. Hands going for his groin. He wasn't immune; he was horny as hell, and she had managed to get her hand into his shorts while he had dodged her mouth. She was fuckable, but as soon as her hands had been on him all he could think about was Emma. He knew Daniel wouldn't care if he fucked Miracle down here; they had shared in the past, and all he needed to do was open a door and bend her over a bed; she was obviously game. He had pushed her off and told her to stay the fuck away; she wasn't what he wanted by a long shot.

* * *

Emma was up on deck when Jake came up from his room, he had been taking a shower in a bid to relax a little. His heart almost stopped when he saw her silhouetted against the railing in a coral bikini and some flimsy wrap around her hips that kept flapping open to reveal long sexy legs. Even for a small girl, her legs looked endless. She was the most perfect sight on and off this boat and everything else paled in comparison when she was around.

Jake was oblivious to Miracle and Marissa's breasts lounging on deck, didn't see anything except Emma and her completely intoxicating body, much more appealing even covered than either of the brunettes. Creamy skin and curves of perfection. He was definitely horny as hell now, just looking at her made his insides want to explode. He wasn't one for self-pleasuring to get sexual gratification but right now, with her in mind, he would happily go back to his room for some release. It had only been a couple of days here and already his constant hard-on was painful. He had been taking cold showers a little too frequently.

Why he had ever thought he could handle Emma in bikinis was beyond him. He should've known it would be hell on earth to be around her and not want to fuck her badly.

"Here." He handed her a bottle of cold, flavored water with a smile, his eyes shielded from view by his Ray-Bans and trying to control every ounce of his body like the expert he was. Years of self-control finally having a use. He was watching that makeup free face and wondering why she ever wore it, she never needed it. Emma was a natural beauty by all standards, flawless perfection.

"Thanks." She opened the bottle with a smile and took a long drink. He had to look away from the way her lips cupped the rim. An internal groan in his head and trying not to picture that mouth doing anything else.

Breathe, Carrero … You're like a horny fifteen-year-old virgin right now.

"You look nice." He focused on her loose hair, his glasses shielding what he was really thinking and trying not to skim her body visually. He needed to disrupt this view somehow and get his head back in the game.

"Thanks." She blushed, and he felt himself frowning, suddenly conscious of the fact she had glanced at his naked upper torso quickly. He was wearing shorts and nothing else and despite never having an issue stripping off in public he suddenly realized why this might be awkward for her. He was still her boss, and he had never been topless in front of her. Not that he was self-conscious in the slightest. He spent enough time in the gym to make sure he was underwear model ready at all times, and his tattoos were always placed in places that enhanced what he had. He was never uncomfortable being naked, especially not in front of women. He felt like an ass for not even thinking that this whole thing might make her uneasy, especially with her background and the way men had treated her. Jake felt like a complete dickhead all of a sudden for not realizing.

"We're going to the shore tonight for dinner … You want to come?" He looked over her head across the water to try to reel in his thoughts, his mood plummeting a little. He had never wanted her to be nervous around him, especially not in this way. He had never thought that maybe Emma's lack of dates this past year had something to do with sex making her uneasy, her childhood had scarred her. Of course, men made her uneasy. He made a mental note at wearing a shirt while walking about on deck, he would make all of them wear one if it made her feel better.

"Sure." She smiled and shielded her eyes from the sun,

Carrero Bonus Book 1 ~ Jake's View

and Jake swiped his shades from his head automatically and placed them on her dainty face.

"I really should carry a pair of these," she laughed, that natural carefree laugh that lifted his mood back up a little, he just shrugged in response. Still mulling over the effect he was obviously having on her. It was like a punch in the stomach, a dull ache that wouldn't shift.

"They look better on you than they do on me. Your cuteness just goes with my shades." Truth be told he never ever thought about putting them on her face, from the first time it had been a natural movement, like breathing. She had shielded her eyes, and he had done it. Something he had done to his kid brother his whole life and somehow, she raised that same protective impulse.

"Where are we going for dinner?" Emma seemed to be looking anywhere but his body and he only frowned harder. He wanted her to be able to stand here with no effect. Well, he wanted him to affect her in a good way but not like this. He wanted to wrap his arms around her right now and tell her it was always going to be okay. He would never let another man touch her, hurt her. He would protect her for eternity. She didn't need to be afraid ever again, it killed him knowing she still carried the burden of those memories.

"Some little seafood place Marissa knows." He tried to keep his tone even at saying her name. He usually avoided any use of the curse word and it felt like broken glass in his mouth.

"I want to get my haircut while we're here … Do you think there are any hairdressers on the mainland?" Jake had the instant urge to tell her she didn't need to change her hair, he liked it the way it was so he looked away toward Leila in hopes of hiding the frown on his face. He didn't like the thought of her changing anything about how she was. You

43

couldn't improve on perfection.

"Leila will know … She comes here a lot." Jake nodded toward his childhood friend, hoping to God Leila wouldn't push Emma into some radical hairdo; he knew her only too well. She was wandering around wearing a top, and for the first time he noticed the other two were not. Completely topless and he suddenly felt pissed. If topless men could make Emma uneasy, then that sure as hell would do it too, he wanted to throw towels over both of them.

"You know Marissa well?" Her voice broke into his thoughts and he felt himself freeze. He had never expected this question to come from her and the last thing he wanted her to know was anything about his past with Marissa. How the hell she had even picked up on anything was beyond him, he sure as hell wasn't putting out any signals where that harpy was concerned.

"Once." He felt his pulse quicken and his head going into evasive mode. He didn't want to dredge up the past and admit he had been too blind to realize his teen girlfriend and best mate had been fucking behind his back and sent him into a few years of booze, drugs, idiotic behavior, and woman. He didn't want Emma knowing that part of him, or tying him to the bitch on deck. He wanted her to see him as he was now, the person he was with her anyway, the better version of himself. He found himself scowling Marissa's way with his back to Emma, Marissa caught his eye and, licking her lips seductively, she squirmed toward him. Even from here he could pick up her *fuck me* signals and he just scowled back.

Not a chance, princess.

"Want to come for a swim with me?" He threw back at Emma. He wanted to get as far away from the slut eyeing him up and away from the topic about her. He needed time alone to help his girl relax. Away from all this naked skin. He turned back to her open expression and had the instant urge to stroke her hair back from her face. His sunglasses did look good on her, a little big but adorably cute.

"Now?" She sounded apprehensive.

"Why not?" Jake smiled, hoping to make her feel more at ease. He needed to get her to unwind a little and he couldn't do that here, tense with a pair of eyes on the back of his head trying to undress him mentally. They needed to leave the past on the deck on her lounger and go find a secluded beach to roam.

"Sure." She smiled brightly, and he could hear Daniel kicking the tunes into a higher gear, looking back to the deck he could see the tell-tale signs of cocaine coming out, and he growled internally. He had fucking warned him against this shit while she was here. He didn't do this crap anymore, and he wasn't going to subject her to it either. He was glad to see Leila wander off deck, knowing she too was out of that whole scene. They had had their young, wild, and reckless days and left them far behind. Daniel needed to catch up. He noted that the twins and their dates seemed into it and put an arm around Emma's shoulders. Guiding her to the side, he waited until she undid her sarong and hung it up before diving in first to make sure he would be in the sea to help her if she needed him when she dove in.

* * *

Being away from them and in the water instantly lightened his mood, her being in here seemed to make her forget about being self-conscious or his naked torso and that made him happier. She smiled and relaxed as they swam and before long he started playfully splashing and pulling her with him. She tried to dunk him under, but he was faster and got her first every time. She seemed to be a pretty competent swimmer, so Jake decided to have a little fun with her before swimming ashore. He had pulled her under with him a few times, enjoying the fact that in the water he could touch her freely without feeling like he was doing something wrong.

"Stop … it." She spluttered to the surface, pleading with him and pushing back her wet hair from her eyes. She looked too cute like this to listen.

"Only if you ask me nicely, tiny tots." He wiped the water from his face, pleased to feel his hair wax was withstanding the sea test. The new lab improvements he had requested were obviously working and Carrero hair wax was now waterproof. He swam to her to close the gap, aware just how naked she really was when he was inches away from molding to her.

"Will you please stop trying to drown me, Mr. Carrero?" She begged, it only made him feel more playful. That adorable little soft voice asking so delicately—she had no chance.

"Seeing as you ask so sweetly, Miss Anderson." He pushed her under again, this time catching her under the water and pulled her back up against him hard. Nose to nose and it didn't seem so right anymore. It was closer than he intended, her body skimming against him in ways that got an immediate hard reaction and he released her quickly. He wasn't sure which part of her body had just rubbed up his groin, but it didn't matter, he was definitely battling down an erection with the efforts of a sumo wrestler right now. He hated that despite all his sexual prowess and years of being a man whore, he couldn't control this shit around her. It was fucking embarrassing.

He swam away from her in an effort to get this under control and put distance between them. He hoped to God she could manage the half mile swim as holding onto her in any way right now would end in an impalement he didn't want to explain.

The beach wasn't that far but it would be exhausting for someone as tiny as her. Jake slowed his pace to make sure he stayed close in case she struggled. He would never let her drown even if he did have to ram a hard-on against her back while rescuing her.

He was glad to find that by the time they hit the beach he had it back under control and mentally chastised himself about getting that close to her again while she was wearing practically nothing. He wandered ahead to let the water drip off and the sun warm and dry his skin in hopes her bikini wasn't showing more than he could handle right now.

God, he needed sex badly.

They wandered around on the beach for a while, the hot sand felt amazing and Jake couldn't help but watch her and those legs strolling around as she picked up shells. So lost in her own head about something, and completely oblivious to him watching her intensely. She was breath-taking in every way, now that her nervousness about being in that pretty mind-blowing bikini seemed to be calming down, he just wanted to stand this way all day and see that little content look on her face. She made him feel all kinds of things right at that moment. Protective, warm, and happy, maybe even a little tug in his heart if he was being honest. He definitely felt horny but not in an overwhelming way like in the water, a more laid-back, gentle attraction. He could handle it this way; if only it would stay this constant.

She stopped and glanced his way, he could feel her eyes before he really saw them as he had taken a moment to wander the shore and breath in some of the surroundings to get his head straight. This was one of his favorite places to kick back after all. Jake loved anything to do with the ocean and being in the great outdoors.

He caught sight of her making her way toward him and turned to watch her walk, the way she moved had always captivated him, graceful, even, and swan-like. At first, she had seemed more stiffly in control over her motions, months ago, but over time she had relaxed. Especially with the ice queen postures and now she was just elegant. Her little nervous habits bugged him though, he hated thinking she ever felt that uneasy around him and whenever he saw her twirling her hair, he wanted to cut her hands off. As soon as he saw those fidgeting fingers, he could never stop the impulsive need to still them.

As soon as she was close enough, he laced her tiny hand in his and tugged her with him. So many times, he had told himself to stop with the touching and hand holding he had started, but he couldn't. It was essential, like breathing and came so naturally with her now that it would be futile. He had started it to get her used to him, long ago when he had first taken her to meet Hunter, he hadn't liked the flinch at his touch, or the fear in those big baby blues. He had made a conscious decision to get her used to his touch if only to relax her and somehow it just grew to this. Holding hands was something he did constantly, pulling her along, hell, even taking her to business meetings. So many times had he caught strange looks from other receptionists that he was pulling his PA along and he would glare back at them. He knew it wasn't normal, but Emma just assumed he was this way with everyone. Margo maybe, not so much hands-on but definitely not everyone. Just people he cared about and always her. Holding her hand now felt right, a perfect fit in the palm of his hand, the familiar soft touch that made him want more from her.

"Here, Emma." He could see her shielding her eyes as the noon sun lifted higher in the sky, so he handed his shades back to her, with her eye color she needed them more than him. He practically spent half his life in the sun and had never really felt any effects from sun glare. Letting her go, he moved along to pick up some pebbles, the sun warming his already brown skin.

"Thanks." She smiled his way as he bent down and expertly skimmed his pebbles across the soft, lapping waves. Looking her way for a moment to gaze on how much more relaxed she seemed away from the others on the boat. Once again, he wished they had come here alone. He wanted nothing more right now.

"What is it?" She tilted her head questioningly at him.

"You seem a bit more relaxed now we're over here." He could definitely see it.

"I feel more relaxed." She sighed and began looking around her feet, pushing the sand with her tiny toes, and looking a bit too squeezable. He took a slow breath and continued skimming stones to distract himself.

"You look it." He skimmed another stone like an expert and was unable to stop the goofy smile hitting his face at watching her.

"I'm glad you made me come." She was watching him more closely now, giving nothing away in that face. Like always.

"I'm glad I didn't have to force you." He grinned, knowing that forcing Emma was never that easy, she had a stubborn streak and was one of the few women he had ever met who stood up to him defiantly. Even when he was being an arsey dickhead. He loved that about her.

"Technically, you gave me no choice." She pouted sassily at him, that tiny little spark that was always beneath the surface. He would love to see her fully let go of it and just turn into a tornado like Leila could. He got the sense she was more than capable but her reserved nature kept it locked down. He wanted to see her release that passion a little. Okay, maybe not to Leila's extent but some of it, anyway. He often wondered if she did it deliberately, kept herself calm and even so she would never lose control.

"You always have a choice with me, Emma, you know that." He looked her way once more, feeling relaxed too, wanting to memorize her standing that way, hands on hips and a body to die for. He shook that mental thought away, knowing that if he stuck with it, his mind would find the shortest route to the gutter again. Being around her minus a whole lot of clothing was trying to say the least, and his libido was starting to fight back.

"We should be getting back; the others will think we don't like them." He tensed and flexed his body, catching a quick glance of her eyes as he did so, and it immediately caught his attention. Definitely no fear that time or any sense of discomfort. That had most definitely been an eye wander of the appreciative female variety—maybe she wasn't as immune as he thought? He would love to explore that possibility. About time his assets were winning her over, he knew he was built and had enough sex appeal. Hell, he knew he was a good-looking bastard, women had made that obvious his whole life.

"Sure, I'm kinda hungry too." She pulled off the shades seemingly shaking it off and handed them back to him, he tried to do the same but that tiny flicker of hope in his chest wouldn't recede back to where it came from. He felt like a girl with all the mushy crap going on inside of him right then and had to chastise himself.

He led the way back into the sea, staying close and making sure the swim back wasn't an ordeal for her. He would have carried her the full way had she seemed tired, but she handled it well. No hint of fatigue, just long, graceful strokes that matched his, and he felt proud of her. She never ceased to impress him.

* * *

They spent lunch on deck with the rest of the party, eating chicken Caesar salad and drinking wine, lounging on the padded double loungers on the main deck. Jake was making sure he stayed by her side and warned his friends off visually. He wouldn't put it past any one of them to make a play for her if he left her alone. Such was the nature of their trips. Each guy always brought dates and some unspoken agreement that all was fair game, and no one would get prissy about it after. The girls they normally brought were bed hoppers, no loyalty and definitely never anyone serious. Leila was the exception normally, she wasn't much for it, and even though he could see she wasn't really that into her date, he knew she wouldn't sleep with any of the others. Emma was completely off limits to any of them, and he would damn well break the neck of any who tried.

Jake was leaning toward Daniel's bed, Emma at his back and in conversation with Leila. Daniel was arguing about sports, one of his passions and Jake just loved to goad him on the matter anytime it came up. He was more into manual stuff, extreme sports he could do himself, but he wasn't against watching the odd football or baseball game. Daniel was just too easy to wind up. He was only half listening though as he could most definitely hear the words "hair" "cut" and "short" going on behind him and he didn't like it one bit.

Looking back at Emma, he caught Leila picking up a strand of that soft honey-blonde hair with the look of someone contemplating cutting it all off. He could feel the frown taking over his face and minor irritation as Leila said, "pixie cut" and he could only assume that was something very short like hers. Emma wouldn't suit Leila's hair, she needed soft and sweet around her face, not edgy and choppy like hers.

"I think you would suit maybe shoulder length." Leila's sweet, little voice was all too sultry, and he could tell she was trying to talk Emma into doing it. That persuasive eye fluttering she had suckered him with many a time in the past twenty years.

"Maybe." Emma picked up a strand too and wound it around her finger, Jake was no longer listening to Daniel at all, he was fully integrated into defending Emma's hair.

"What's wrong with how it is?" He frowned, keeping his hands down and quelling the urge to run his fingers over the strand she was holding. She suited her wavy halo of soft hair, it was feminine and her. He didn't like the idea of no longer having it hanging down her back and blowing gently in the breeze.

"Jake? Men have no clue. Women like a drastic change every so often." Leila quipped at him with that sassy raised brow and he just wanted to sit on her right about now.

"If it's not broke, then don't fix it." He bit back, he was used to these little head to heads with this short fiery devil. He would be damned if she was going to push his Emma around.

"Maybe it's not broken but can definitely be revamped. Women do like to shake it up every so often. Try on a new look." Leila was putting on her sarcastic tone, raising that brow and challenging him, yet again. This girl never ceased to push his buttons and sometimes he wondered why the hell he hadn't just drowned her in the past.

"It's my hair!" Emma cut in, raising hands between the two in a bid to distract them but she wasn't swaying these two. This was a common thing, Leila and Jake head-on in subtle ways, always finding something to challenge one another over. It was just how they were.

"I like it how it is. If you want to change it then fine, it can always grow back." Jake felt stupid as his tone came out, he sounded more like Emma's boyfriend than her boss about now and Leila was smirking. The urge to push her face into the lounger was strong; if she still had pigtails he was sure he would tie them over her mouth right now.

"Worried your girlfriend won't get you all hot and bothered with short hair, Jacob?" Leila leaned over Emma and prodded him in the shoulder. He just scowled back at her, she was pushing her luck today. He could easily pick her up and throw her overboard.

"Shut up, wench. Emma has more sense than to let me be her boyfriend."

And didn't he know it?

"Oh right, I forgot. You're just friends." The honey-like way she said it made him grimace a smile her way, clenched teeth and warning her off with his eyes. He could see that glint of cheeky amusement and really did wonder why Mrs. Huntsberger didn't smack Leila more as a child. "I can see that," she added sarcastically, and he wondered if spanking her now would make any difference.

"Really, we are." Emma sounded quiet, flustered, and he tried to ignore the crazy going off inside of him, trying not to react badly to something he already knew. He should have been used to her subtle rejections by now.

"Well then, you won't care if I take her to get it all shorn off then, will you?" Leila threw a defiant look his way and he bit his tongue in a bid to stop bickering, frowning, and glaring. As soon as he got her alone he was going to chew her head off.

Devilish little minx, she knew exactly what she was doing.

"Emma can do whatever she wants with her hair. She'll always look beautiful." He got up, walking away before he made good and sat on Leila and tried to pull her ears off or something equally immature.

Brat.

"Someone is not a happy little playboy today!" He heard her say, even though he was moving away to the buffet table and ignored her.

Witch!

No, he's fucking not. Last thing he wants is Emma changing, she was perfect the goddamn way she already was!

* * *

After lunch, Jake took Leila and Emma ashore on the speedboat kept moored to the cruiser, any excuse to get that thing out on open waters and let rip. He hoped she wasn't going to come back with some crazy short hair but what could he do? He had no right to say anything. He wasn't her boyfriend, just her boss and as much as he invaded her life at times, he knew where the boundaries lay.

They met the car and driver he had waiting at the port and handed Emma his credit card. That immediate frown on her face and her mouth pouting to verbalize a refusal was shot down with his no-nonsense glare. She knew his looks all too well and seemed to think better than pushing her luck on this front. He had warned her enough times at work that this trip was being financed by him and if she argued about it, then there would be hell to pay. He had been raised that way, and it wasn't just about taking care of her, it was about his ego too. Emma slid it into her bag gracefully, she had used this card for ordering things for him at work, so she was more than capable of using it now.

He pushed away the urge to kiss her on the cheek, with Leila hovering he knew that it would just raise more knowing eyebrows and he knew for a fact Leila was the type to point out to Emma that he had the major hots for her. He had kept his cool this far and thrown everyone off the scent, and he was sure as hell not letting Leila get her teeth into that little-known fact. Emma would run for the hills if she knew how he really felt about her.

He watched them go before putting the boat into reverse and backing away from the pier. She was in the red dress today and much as he tried not to look at her this way, he couldn't help it. She was irresistible in every way and only so much more in floaty, girly clothes that had made an appearance on this trip. God, he would keep her this way all the time if he could. As much as he loved her office outfits, and he surely did, this much sexy was hotter than hell, he liked this far more. She looked like the kind of girl you married like this, perfect, angelic, soft, and he wanted nothing more than to walk around showing her off.

Back at the boat Jake headed to his room and pulled off his T-shirt. While Emma was on shore he was going to kick back, swim some, and spend some time with Danny and the twins, having a beer and catching up. He knew that Marissa and Miracle were afternoon nappers, unlike Emma and Leila, and wouldn't show face for a while at this time of the day. He hated lazy women who partied late and then lounged all day with nothing else in their lives. Emma had more get up and go than that, even hungover she still dragged her ass to work and rarely complained. He could never imagine someone like her ever being happy with the lifestyle Marissa was effortless at. Spoiled rich bitch with nothing to do all day except work on a tan.

He made his way to the deck and found Daniel already on a lounger, topless with a beer in hand and the twins splashing around in the ocean trying to drown one another. Jake moved to the next lounger and sat down heavily, Hunter automatically grabbing a beer from the cooler beside him and tossing it to Jake. He opened it and downed half. Drinking in the sun was pretty dumb, but he had done it for years and it never affected him like it used to.

"So, the little women off to abuse your accounts?" Daniel smirked his way, and Jake just nodded his head at him.

"Probably." He shrugged and sat back, easing his body onto the padded bed fully and lifting his legs, kicking his trainers off the side. Leila would definitely encourage Emma to abuse his credit card and he hoped she would.

"What's the deal with you and her? Don't give me that *friends* bullshit line again man ... It's pretty obvious she's under your skin." Daniel lifted his shades and looked at Jake pointedly, scrutinizing his face with that intense Hunter glare.

"I'll be fucked if I know. As much as I tell myself I have a handle on this ... I don't." He sighed. He had never lied to Danny, in all the years they had been friends, brutal honesty was always their thing, and he knew he could trust him to never breathe a word to anyone else. Hunter was a lot of things, but a loyal tried and tested best mate above all. Surprisingly wise when he saw fit and not against love despite his own aversion to it.

"Being honest here, mate ... I've never seen you this way over any chick, what's so goddamn special about this one?" Daniel frowned his way, genuine curiosity across his face.

"Everything ... Nothing ... Fuck knows. She's her. I can't pinpoint it—just from the minute she walked into my office I wasn't me ... No control, zero ability to function properly, and the longer I know her the worse it is." Jake was stressed talking about this, he had never analyzed it, he tried not to.

"There must be something specific?" Daniel was maneuvering his position to stare at Jake more fully, going in for the shrink's approach it appeared. He did seem genuinely curious.

"Which specific thing do I pick ... How she looks? How she is? How she makes me feel? ... She's Emma, she's not got anything about her that's not great. Except maybe the not wanting me part." Jake hunched his shoulders and scrubbed a hand down his face.

"Maybe that's it ... Maybe because she's probably the first woman in the history of Carrero to actually not want to jump your bones?" Daniel said smugly, and Jake considered it for a moment.

"I genuinely used to tell myself that exact thing." He sighed.

"You're suffering from some sort of bruised ego, man, chick turned you down flat and doesn't want the great Carrero boner. It's reverse psychology or some shit. If she was all over you, then maybe you wouldn't be interested."

Daniel grinned but Jake knew this was wrong, as much as he wanted to tell himself Daniel could have a point. Maybe in the beginning but not now. He knew that having her once wouldn't take away this need. If he was right, he would want a one-night stand, and he didn't. He wanted something meaningful with her.

"I wish you were right." He grimaced, at least Daniel's idea had some sort of resolution.

"It's a crush, something you don't ever get ... You obviously think she's beyond hot and your picky ass self doesn't normally find that in a girl," Daniel said.

"She's beautiful. Perfect even." Jake shrugged this time, he meant every word.

"Okay, bit strong on that front, she's cute, I'll give you that, but she's not really like mind-blowingly beautiful." Daniel waved an airy hand his way and Jake instantly growled back.

Daniel had to be kidding right now.

"Are you blind?" Jake was defensive, skin prickling with almost instant aggression at anyone tearing Emma down.

"Come on? I mean she's hot, I get it ... She's ... She's not Leila hot. Leila is my idea of a beautiful girl." Daniel averted his eyes to the rail of the boat, evasive anytime his own emotions came into play.

"Don't even go there, you know that subject just pisses me off because you're an asshole." Jake frowned a warning and the hostile change of tone rendered them both silent for a moment. Daniel finally shifted uncomfortably. That topic was a long-done deal and history had proven they couldn't talk about Leila without a heated fight soon after.

"You know, maybe you just need to get laid, this isn't like you at all ... How long has it been? I'm sure your balls are probably blue by now and it would account for the moody assed nature." He laughed, and Jake just threw him an amused frown. Daniel was a dick.

"I lost count, it all became pretty mind-numbingly painful after a week and now it seems like years." He sighed and drunk more beer, pulling his shades down to cover his eyes when facing the sun this way.

"Just fuck someone and at least release some tension. Marissa is giving you the all hot and ready signs and as much as I'm against you going down that route again, I am not against you abusing her body. It's still fucking fit ... Miracle wouldn't say no either, and that chick takes it in every way. Her ass is pretty fine too." Daniel laughed dirtily, and Jake only sighed again. He wasn't in the mood for picturing sex right now, his body was barely holding on.

"I think not ... On both accounts. I don't need to complicate this shit more than I am." He sat up agitated, a stirring in his groin at the sex talk and for a moment contemplated heading down to Miracle's room and seeing what she could do with her mouth. Emma's mouth came into his mind's eye and he slumped back down in irritation, all urges of any other woman evaporating.

For the love of God, she was infiltrating every part of his head nowadays.

"So, fuck it, put the moves on her properly. This pussy shit you're doing is not the Carrero I know and love. You're wimping out big time over this chick. Just swoop in like you always do and get her naked and screaming in under five minutes." Daniel hauled another beer out and threw a second to Jake, he caught it swiftly and propped it against his short-covered hip.

"I can't ... She's not like that. She doesn't do one-night

stands and then what? I still have to work with her." Jake was starting to feel agitated, the tight ache in his lower stomach growing and he couldn't decide if it was irritation or something else. He had the horn, he needed to fuck someone. Daniel was right on that front. He was a hot-blooded guy with a high sex drive and he had never put himself into self-inflicted celibacy in his life.

"The way you're acting, Jake, I don't think one night would be your goal … You're totally pussy whipped over this chick and you know it. Suck it up and just go all in for her." Daniel was smirking his way again, and this time he needed a moment to just think. Daniel was right. He wouldn't be happy with a onetime thing with her, he knew the second he had her he would want more. He knew it so painfully that it had stopped him ever trying. She didn't want this and, to be honest, having her outright reject him would be agony.

He looked out over the water at the ripples on the surface from the twins and sighed.

"Unrequited … That's a word I never thought I'd hear myself using … Especially in terms of it being me on the painful side." He smarted and rubbed the bridge of his nose with his thumb, avoiding Daniel's eyes.

"Jesus, man, what girl could resist you? You're a handsome fuck and way too sexy for most women to handle. Have you ever just asked her?" Daniel sprayed beer his way, and he snapped his face back, ready to beat him over the head with something in an instant anger spike.

"Fuck off, wanker." He wiped the spray off his arm and contemplated chucking his unopened can at Hunter's face as payback. Ruining that pretty smile would be entertaining.

"Seriously, though?" Daniel smirked at him, a bit too obnoxiously.

"No. There's no point, I know her. She gives me nothing. No signals, no hints, no tiny mannerisms to even suggest she would be interested. Emma is completely immune to me in every way and it fucking sucks." He put his can down and crossed his arms over his head to block out the light. He wasn't enjoying this conversation at all and Daniel seemed to be enjoying it a little too much.

"Then why the fuck are you celibate? She has no hold over you, she's not making you wait with any fly teasing or hints of more … Fuck someone and end this misery." Daniel leaned out and pushed him aggressively.

He couldn't explain it, he was already so messed up over this. He just knew that it was pointless. If he even got close to a woman that wasn't her, he knew for a fact his dick would cease to cooperate, he had a mental block and until she got out of the way he was stuck this way.

"If I could I would!" he snapped back. "Look, man, can we just drop this shit, I'm seriously not in the mood for this and it's ruining my calm." He sulked, childish Carrero on play and he didn't give a shit right now. Hunter was used to all versions of him.

"Right … as your best mate, I'm doing you a favor. Stay put." Jake kept his eyes closed and arms over his face and just ignored him. Whatever plan he was hatching Jake wasn't interested. He heard Daniel slide up and pace off toward the other end of the deck and sighed. Reaching over to Daniel's lounger he picked up the iPod left there and stuck the headphones in. When Hunter came back he was killing this conversation, it was pointless and going nowhere fast. Rehashing his feelings wasn't going to make a damn bit of difference. He switched on the playlist and was immediately blasted with Nickelback, Hunter's favorite band right now, and went back to covering his face with his arms. He was tired from last night's late one, maybe a nap would put him in a better mood while she was away.

* * *

It felt like only seconds later when in the darkness a warm, moist sensation ran down his abdomen toward his shorts' waist making his muscles tense in a really good way, in his dream-like state he pictured Emma running her tongue down his body and smiled. He could picture her doing exactly that as it felt much like he would expect a small warm tongue to feel. Moving south, the sensation twirled around his waistband and he squirmed sleepily.

God, she was good with her tongue.

He could picture her soft blue eyes looking up at him sexily and he was definitely getting hard with it. His waistband was tugged slightly, and he felt himself heating up with the dream, fucking her in his sleep was common but this was a new turn, never had he dreamed about her blowing him off and he sure as hell wasn't about to stop it. He was aware that his brain was trying to wake him up, but he fought it to hold on to the pictures in his head. He didn't care if he had a wet dream lying here, she had given him plenty in the past months and Daniel sure as hell wouldn't laugh. All guys did it.

That hot, warm mouth moved lower, pulling his shorts down enough to get the tip of him free and connected with a suction that almost made him come right then. Suddenly realizing this was all a little too un-Emma and feeling a little too real had him sitting up with a start and blinking at his surroundings harshly. He looked down at the still warm sensation encircling his dick and scowled at the brunette with her face in his lap, before shoving her away hard. He sent

Miracle, who was fully naked, sliding across the deck aggressively and unceremoniously.

Fuck!

"What the fuck are you doing?" he barked at her, pulling himself right and jumping to his feet. He felt dirty … like he needed a shower all of a sudden. "And put some fucking clothes on." He snapped again, lifting the towel from Hunter's lounger and throwing it at her as he saw the tears in her eyes. A look of complete shock and humility, not that he could blame her. Old Carrero would have been more than open to this little scenario only a couple of months ago. Hell, he would have helped it along and taken his shorts off and pulled her onto his lap impatiently.

God damn, Daniel!

This was Hunter's idea of helping him? Getting his porn star sidekick to blow him off while he was asleep and, judging by the nakedness, she had intended climbing on top when he was turned on. The thought made him feel sick. If he hadn't woken up, he would have fucked her. God, if his sleep condition had kicked in he would definitely have done it and not exactly in a good way. Like that he was aggressive and fevered and had been known to screw like a caveman with zero control.

Did she even have a goddamn condom with her? Or did she just assume climbing onto him bareback was fucking acceptable because she was a porn star who obviously used birth control?

The thought made his skin crawl, porn stars had never been his type. He liked his women with fewer air miles, so to speak. He wanted to lash out right now, find Hunter and beat him. He was so unbelievably pissed off.

The girl just sat cowering at his temper, clutching the towel across her breasts pointlessly, still as much on show at

Jake & Emma

his unexpected reaction, he felt guilty and held out a hand to help her up when she just continued to stare at him.

"Look, I'm sorry, okay. Just don't do shit like that. If I wanted to fuck you, then you sure as hell would know about it. I don't. I'm here with Emma." She hesitated, then let him pull her to her feet, using the towel a little more successfully and sniffing back a tear. Big doe eyes on show and his temper calming. Girls were hard to be mad at when they did all that vulnerable shit.

"Daniel told me to surprise you, said once I started, you would blow my mind." She bit on her lip and he felt the rest of the anger dissipate at the childish mannerism Emma had too.

"Daniel's a prick. You can tell him I said so." Jake clicked his neck to release the tension and waved her away. Hoping to God she would never try this crap again. He would need to sleep with one eye open or just sleep beside Emma anytime he needed a nap if Hunter was hell-bent on curing his celibacy.

Wanker.

"Go, leave me to cool down and don't bring this up again, okay?" He would be having some fucking stern words with Hunter; this shit was not on at all. He noticed how the sneaky bastard had never reappeared. With his woman up here, he was probably screwing the other slut down below. Not that he cared. Marissa had had more men than hot dinners in the last decade and Daniel would use and abuse her in any way he saw fit.

The more degraded the better.

"Pussy." Hunter's voice carried from behind, and he saw him rising up the ladder from the sea, asshole was swimming not screwing. Rare for him. Mind you, despite all his leering at Marissa he knew Daniel hated her with a passion, maybe enough to bypass sex.

"Fuck off … What the hell was that?" Jake moved at him angrily, temper reigniting at his presence and Daniel feigned a submissive position. Flapping hands like a woman.

"Please don't hit me, big boy." He whimpered in a girly voice with fluttering lashes, kissy lips on top of it all.

Jesus, why was this moron his friend?

"Prick." Jake dove in, grappling Hunter around the waist and pulling him into a wrestling hold on the deck floor. Hunter was quick to fight back and soon they were knocking lumps out of each other and rolling around like idiots. Jake got Hunter with an elbow to the jaw, a muffled grunt before the twins appeared.

"Get a room, pansies," Vince smirked as he stalked by, dodging the leg that came out to kick him.

"Jealous much?" Daniel pouted from the headlock Jake had him in before Jake shoved him away and punched him in the shoulder a little forcefully. Asshole needed to learn some manners.

Daniel threw him a glare and tried to flick him in the face, Jake dodged easily with his lightning reflexes and jumped to his feet as Richard climbed the last rung onto the boat too.

"Lovebirds at it again?" Richard smirked at his twin and he nodded back. The two of them were like a double act, not a funny one though just a couple of assholes. Jake turned to Hunter with a frown.

"Don't ever pull that shit again … If I wanted a blow job I would go down and demand one," he fumed, but both twins just broke into huge grins.

"What have we missed here? Hunter, did you finally

Jake & Emma

embrace your Jake love and try to give the man a BJ?" Vincent burst into hysterical laughter and Daniel only shook his head.

"Ha funny ha, fuck off … He turned down Miracle … Laugh it up, dickheads." Daniel stuck his fingers up at the pair, lifting a towel from the bed and throwing it at them.

"Why would he want your cast-offs when he has that tight assed little thing looking all fuck-me-now wandering around? I would tap that ass over Miracle any day." Vincent grinned but Jake's temper flared.

"Knock it the fuck off … Don't speak about her like that. *Ever*!" Jake was growling, full-on fierce protector and he didn't want them talking about her like she was some piece of meat. He didn't want them even breathing her way, let alone thinking of touching her.

"Ahhhhh … Jake's in lurve." Richie threw a beer toward him and he caught it mid-air. A grip that almost caused it to explode on impact.

"Jake's not fucking impressed with this conversation so can we just drop it?" He glared at both of them, opening his can while Hunter had the sense to wander off and collapse on a lounger, getting the bed damp with the water still clinging to him.

Jake was not in love … Okay, maybe Jake could be in love, but he shouldn't be because this was going nowhere and had heartbreak written all over it.

"What's she like in the sack?" Vincent threw a look his way, but Jake only growled in response. All tension returned, body prickling and ready to start boxing for real.

"Leave him alone, can't you see he has zero sense of humor when it comes to Emma?" Daniel cut in and the warning look he was throwing off matched Jake's. He may be

Carrero Bonus Book 1 ~ Jake's View

a twat and a half, but Daniel didn't like anyone else giving his best mate a hard time. It was his job alone. Jake was relieved to see the twins take the warning, one thing about them was they respected Hunter's word. Jake wasn't with the twins often enough anymore to have the same hierarchy with them that Hunter did, he was losing his edge and getting soft according to them nowadays. He should beat the shit out of them and show them he was still as much Alpha as Hunter was. Beat them for even daring to mention Emma in a derogatory way.

"I think everyone should just chill the fuck out and crack open the beer." Daniel lifted an eyebrow his way and Jake softened. Drinking was a sure-fire way to calm him down right now and he was game. Emma would be hours yet and if he slept before she came back he would be sober enough to withstand her.

* * *

Being sober at some point had been the plan but as the day had worn on the men had kept on drinking beers, they had swum, headed to the private beach he'd taken Emma to and played a little netball, ran around like kids for a while, and they had pretty much eaten nonstop most of the afternoon.

He had kept checking his watch, wondering what she was doing and hoping she was having a good time with Leila. Not that he should worry, Leila was a good time girl and sweet enough to make Emma feel right at home. He just wished she was here right now, he missed her.

He was too drunk to drive the speed boat ashore when the day drew on and had the ship's crew taxi them instead, Emma had been gone all day and he had quelled the urge to call her and text her a dozen times. The merrier he had got the stronger the urge to just have her right here in his arms, beside him with that intoxicating little face and perfect smell.

Smell? Jesus, he really was in trouble … Knowing her smell was pretty much admitting in neon lights to himself that he was in love with her. What guy associated a girl with how she smelled and actually ached for it? Fuck.

He was in so much trouble with her.

Miracle kept her distance on the boat ride, but Marissa was borderline humping his leg much to the un-amusement of her date. Vincent was watching her with a face that just yelled "Tramp" at her. Poor guy should have realized this would happen, there was a reason all their trips had a "No Marissa" rule and he had stupidly broken it. She was like a dog on heat whenever she got within a fifty-mile radius of Jake, had been for years.

Apart from one drunken fuck-up that he had no memory of last month, he had never gone down that route and never would again. Even if she hadn't broken his heart years ago, she was a coldhearted manipulative bitch that he would have seen through eventually. She was the exact opposite of Emma in every way. Not just in looks but in body and soul. Emma was pure and good in every way that Marissa was dark and nasty. He shrugged her away and moved forward enough in the hopes that they would get ashore before he let go and threw her overboard.

The restaurant was nice and private, it had a beach theme and little palm leaf roofs over each table that made it quirky and relaxed. The tables spilled out onto the sand near the shore and were strung with fairy lights now it was getting dull. Not that Jake cared, his mind was on one thing only. Jake couldn't help but keep watching for Emma's arrival, he'd text them when they were on the way here knowing a phone call would only have his so-called mates crooning in the background. He was missing her crazily, it felt like she had been gone for days already and a part of him was nervous that he would hate her new hair.

He swore, not one of them better say anything about the day's conversation.

Marissa was making a hell of a play at trying to get him into some eye on eye action, he had no idea what was with this chick. No patience for the way she was trying to catch his attention when they all picked seats, so he decided to stay on his feet as far from her as he could manage. Last thing he needed was Emma arriving and seeing Marissa eye humping him when he really wanted to avoid all talk of her.

Daniel stayed upright too, coming to his side as the twins ordered in the first round of drinks at the bar. Miracle was sitting next to Marissa, avoiding him at all costs and obviously still embarrassed about earlier, it was obvious the two didn't exactly get on but were making conversation out of boredom. Marissa was still watching him a little too hawkishly. He wished she would just fuck off.

The twins came back with trays and started dispersing glasses and bottles all over the table, Jake was handed a beer, Daniel already unsteady on his feet was a sign that maybe he should stop drinking. Daniel had the same tolerance as him, and they had pretty much stayed level in the amount they had drunk all day. If he could see signs of it in Hunter, then he was sure he was probably worse than he realized too, and drunk Jake would be no good at behaving himself around Emma. She was too much of a lure for wandering eyes, hands and mouths.

Jake pushed Hunter playfully as he swayed closer and banged into him for the third time.

Jake & Emma

"Jesus, man … stop trying to cuddle up to me." He smirked at him and Daniel just shoved him back.

"You're the one who's trying it on with me, all this lack of playtime has you thinking bro sex is acceptable." Hunter just smirked right back cheekily at him as the two twins decide to stay standing too, the four of them forming a little group on the side of the table and ostracizing both women.

"Never, ever would that be acceptable." Richard cringed, and Jake just shook his head at him.

"Says the guy who slept naked in a womb with another bloke for nine months and most likely a bed for the first few more." Jake pointed his bottle at him with a cheeky smile. Jake had no problem with gay men, he knew and liked a few of them but his immediate circle of friends right now was obviously not as comfortable with it.

"Yeah, I reckon Vince is the big spoon and Richie here takes it like a trooper … Brotherly love and all that." Hunter laughed, amused by his own jokes. Jake smiled too, taking a swig of his mellow beer and watching them closely.

"Shut the fuck up … I am not that way inclined!" Richie made an effort at putting on a manly pose and grabbed at his package crudely. "I'm all horny male for tits and ass."

"Notice he said ass … Not pussy?" Daniel frowned Jake's way, they clinked beer bottles across the neck with nods of agreement. Riling your mates was the best amusement a guy could get.

"Busted, little brother, now bend over and take it like a good little bitch!" Vince tried to push him forward but was only met with a flustered and almost angry Richie slapping him away.

"Shut up or I'll tell them about that tramp you let use a strap-on up your ass." Richie spat at his brother and then laughed when Vincent turned crimson. Only reinforcing the fact he had done that. Both Jake and Daniel grimaced at the thought and looked at one another as if to say "Yeah ... just NO." As kinky as both of them were when it came to sex even they drew the line on some things. Anal on a guy was one of those things, although he was pretty sure if Emma was ever up for that sort of thing he would do it to her.

Mind out of the gutter, Carrero ... She's too pure for that shit.

Jake glanced in the direction of approaching blonde hair for a moment, some inner sense to turn that way, then did a double take when he realized that small blonder wavy-haired girl was in fact Emma. And she looked fucking amazing.

Holy hell.

Her hair had been cut to above shoulder length, somehow the waves had only gotten wilder and sexier being shorter, blonder highlights which lightened her honey-blonde and framed that perfect face in a way that just made every single nerve in his body react impulsively. She was beyond stunning.

Man, he wanted to fuck her right now. Badly.

He quelled the urge to groan, reeling back in the five thousand filthy thoughts running through his head right now and walked toward her. She was locked on him visually, smiling softly and completely inviting. For a second, he could have sworn she had missed him too if her expression was anything to go by. Without even thinking, he was drawn straight to touching that hair, pushing back a strand from her face and reveling in how soft it felt between his fingers.

How soft she looked, how she smelled.

God, he had missed her like crazy and right now she was like some perfect vision of angelic beauty captivating him and knocking everything else out of focus around them as she smiled up at him almost adoringly. The urge to kiss her was killing him. He ran his hand through that touchable hair and concentrated on staying in control as much as he could. Realizing just how close to her he had gotten and cooled his heavy breathing so she wouldn't see how much he was unraveling. He really needed to sober up if he was going to stop himself.

"I like this. A lot!" He said softly, his eyes heavy with lust and intoxication and knowing being this drunk this close to her was a bad idea, he was fighting with every piece of his strength to not just lean down the rest of the way and kiss her. Her mouth was just calling to be kissed right now, soft, pouted and free of makeup and achingly inviting. He could almost reach her, taste her and he knew she would taste as good as she smelled.

"Thank you." She smiled, sexy soft-voiced and pulled the hair from his hand, tucking it back with the rest of her short waves shyly. Eyes flooring him in that way she sometimes looked at him that almost convinced him he stood a chance with her. She looked so goddamn adorable when she was like this and he had zero control. He leaned down almost losing the battle to stop himself from kissing her and at the last moment caught it and redirected it to her cheek.

Close, Carrero … So, fucking close.

He needed to have more control than this, he needed to sober up a little if he was going to have to look at her all night in that dress and new very fuckable hair. He had been wrong about her cutting it, as much as he had loved it the way it was this somehow was more her. Made her a hundred times more appealing even though he had never been one for shorter hair. It was softer, sexier yet still angelic and he loved it.

Grasping her hand to ground himself back to reality he

looked back at those perfect baby blue eyes which only somehow seemed bigger and softer with all the layers around her face. Jesus his girl was probably the most breathtaking woman he had ever known, and it was taking the strength of a hundred men not to lift her up around his waist right now and devour her. It was almost painful to just take her hand when every fiber of his body was aching for more.

"Come on." He entwined her small delicate fingers in his, happier than hell to have her back with him again and led her proudly to the table. She was the most beautiful woman in the bistro and he would be damned sure no one else was going to get a look in at her. He wouldn't be held liable for having to endure some other guy making a play for her, she would see a violence come out of him that would probably send her running for the hills. Emma followed obediently, tightening her hand in his snugly and making him feel like the only thing that mattered right now was that tiny little set of fingers wrapped in his. She felt like home.

* * *

They sat outside under palm frond umbrellas and the food was pretty good, it helped Jake to sober up enough to not want to haul Emma down the beach and molest her. They had all moved on to drinking cocktails thanks to Leila and her crazy huge knowledge on all things cocktail. The girl had once run a little bar somewhere exotic for fun a few years back and seemed to retain the recipe of every drink known to man. She was always handy in teaching Jake new drinks to impress the ladies and right now his knowledge of Emma's preferences was helping him keep her in a steady supply of drinks she was happily downing. He liked seeing her relax this way, sitting beside him and fully leaning back in her chair without any hint of defensiveness.

He was more than aware of the way the three of his so-called friends were honing in on Emma with her new hair, warning glares at them had proven futile and Daniel smirking was a hint that he was heating up to start trying to goad Jake. The guy got a kick out of it. Jake shifted uneasily ready to defend her with his life if that's what it took, he wouldn't let any of them make even a tiny hint at trying for her.

"What motivated this?" Daniel reached past Jake, scooping a strand of Emma's hair and Jake batted his hand away aggressively.

"No touching." The scowl was somewhere between funny and serious and very impulsive. Daniel just raised an eyebrow and grinned at him knowingly, Jake wasn't amused in the slightest at what Hunter was playing at.

"Sorrryyy, big man. You have to admit though, your girl does look extra hot with this new do." He winked at Emma and Jake had to push down the urge to kick him in the face from this angle. If he thought he could flirt with her to get at him then he better back off. Jake's years of mixed martial arts and boxing meant even from a seated position he could take his head off his shoulders. Best mate or not there was a line Daniel shouldn't cross, for Jake it would always be her.

"Umm, thanks." Emma cut in blandly, watching the way Jake frowned at Daniel then punched him lightly in the shoulder. He was trying to curb the aggression but still warn Daniel to back off.

"She's not going to sleep with you, so you can cut out the compliments and the flirty crap." Jake huffed Hunter's way with a scowl.

"Oh, I don't know. I reckon I could charm Miss Ander

Carrero Bonus Book 1 ~ Jake's View

… OWWW." Daniel squawked like an injured animal as Jake shoulder punched him a lot harder. Fist connecting with the bone under the muscle and most definitely warning him off. "Calm your pants, Jake. God! You'll be pissing on me next." He huffed and swiped his beer from the table.

"Don't tempt me." Jake wasn't kidding, he wanted to send a clear message to all three men that YES, he had zero humor when it came to her and they all better learn that fast. Daniel and Jake threw angry looks at one another before taking what looked like precision planned swigs of their drinks.

"Jeez, testosterone flying much?" Leila laughed, pulling some of the tension away.

"Men!" Emma sighed in exasperation, glancing Jake's way with amusement before joining Leila in an eyebrow raise. Jake felt his jets cooling at just watching her interact with Leila. He wanted her to have a friend in her, she was his best girl mate and they were well suited. It helped soothe his hot temper a little.

"Needless to say, I was right!" Leila grinned at Emma with some underlying message between the two girls and Jake found himself narrowing eyes on them.

What now?

"About what?" Marissa cut in with a pinched tone that made both women look her way with rather snooty expressions. She was sprawled at the table with full cleavage on show, right in Jake's eye line and making it obvious it was intentional. He swigged on his beer and looked away. Miracle was picking her nails at the right of her in a similar pose, seemingly a new-found love of Jake all of a sudden and he felt himself eye roll and looked back to Emma.

Women!

Jake & Emma

"That Jake would be enamored with her new short do … That she would look sexy as hell!" Leila's triumphant tone made Marissa eye roll and Jake had the urge to pour her cocktail over her head. Even for a girl with pretty features, a nice body and generally attractive, he found her repulsive. That black heart and snooty face just killed any looks she once had.

"Jake's a man! He appreciates it when women try really hard to get a reaction from him." Marissa said icily with a flick of her hair, Jake glared at her harshly, not liking her dig at Emma one bit. She glared back challenging him and he had to hold his tongue.

"You would know!" Leila's scathing comment came with a new tone for her. Disdain. Jake couldn't agree more though, if anyone needed a crown for trying to get Jake's attention then it was Marissa. Emma didn't need to try at all. Jake caught sight of the twins moving uneasily in their chairs and both men lift drinks to focus on that instead. Miracle lifted her head in interest, eyes gleaming with the possibility of drama. He sighed knowing the signs of trouble brewing and he wouldn't let any of them ruin this for her.

"Emma doesn't need to vie for my attention. She already has it, and her hair is a knockout. Much like her." Jake cut in smoothly, his glare fixed on Marissa coldly, that sinister tone in his voice, devoid of emotion yet portraying a lot to the people who knew him, and everyone hushed up. He hoped to God his dangerous tone and angry scowl gave everyone the message to back off. He used to be the Alpha of this little circle and he sure as hell would be taking that title back if they kept this shit up.

"Man, did it just get cold in here?" Daniel jumped up from his perch on the edge of the table and slapped Jake on the back. "We need a new topic and way more booze, man."

Carrero Bonus Book 1 ~ Jake's View

Daniel was toeing the line, taking his place in the hierarchy and glances toward the twins saw them shuffling their feet too.

"Couldn't agree more." Jake relaxed back, happy with the sudden submissive atmosphere. Marissa and Miracle looking down at their fingernails. Jake feeling better, he leaned in and kissed the oblivious Emma on the cheek spontaneously, giving Marissa that back off signal as much as the rest of them. She maybe wasn't his woman in the normal sense, but she was his queen while on this boat and they would damn well treat her that way.

* * *

It didn't take much to get the happy jovial atmosphere back, and Jake relaxed into his usual sociable self. Happy that everyone was having a relatively good time and even Marissa seemed to be backing off and occasionally smiling.

Emma had never seen him surrounded by people he could relax with and even though the group was small he was kicking back as much as she was. He had tried to slow down his alcohol consumption and was not any drunker than he had been, although Emma was definitely getting tipsy. He had never laughed so much at her in the whole time he had known her. She was cute drunk, funny and less guarded. She giggled like a child and lost all the airs and graces she sometimes hid behind. Jake loved Emma like this. As though it was like getting a glimpse of who she could be if she ever really did feel comfortable enough to fully let her guard down around him and he wished she was like this more of the time.

She seemed to get on with Leila effortlessly, and he was

glad that out of all the girls here she had chosen her. They gelled, and it was nice to see because he knew Leila was one of the few decent girls who was genuine in this lifestyle. She would stick up for her and defend her with honesty if the catty other two started that shit again.

Jake hauled her up to dance when the band came out and it was pretty obvious Emma had gone beyond tipsy. He had danced with her a million times at events and never had she been this useless. He couldn't stop laughing and having to grab onto her to support her every two seconds as she kept falling off her shoes. She was all over the place and even when he pulled her against him suggestively she somehow ended up teetering all over the place unable to stop swaying. The temptation to wrap his arms around her fully and put her on top of his shoes so she could stay at peace was killing him. She was so much sexier like this, fully trusting in him to put hands on her wherever he saw fit, but he was trying to be a gentleman. So hard to do when the girl was grabbing his hands and pulling them to her body in a way too sexy dance, the drunker she got. Emma was outright flirting with him now she was drunk, and he wanted nothing more than to just stop caring and go with it.

"Your moves are terrible when you're plastered, shorty." He spun her around, catching her from the back and pulling her against him. Hips swaying in time and his arms firmly around her, he knew he had to get them off this dance floor before the gentleman in him fucked off completely.

"Shhhh. I'm doing just fine." She slurred playfully. Giggling at him and just making him smile all the more.

God, he loved her.

"Sure, you are. The second I let go, you'll facepalm the deck. I'm all that's keeping you upright." He joked with her, her hair was just under his chin and smelled like tropical fruit and her and just made him want to taste her all the more.

"I'm sure I wouldn't … You're exaggerating my drunkenness." She purred demurely, turning in his arms and giving him a gentle chest shove. "Let me go and see." She challenged him and that inner boy of his lifted his hands with a shrug and a smile and stepped back to leave her to it and prove a point. She attempted a step away sassily and stumbled over her own heels immediately, Jake's quick reflexes catching her and pulling that delicate curvy body into his with a tug to save her. He had to steel the surge of lust at pulling every one of them damn curves against him so fully.

"You were saying?" He smiled at her and let her loose a little.

"Shut up." Emma toppled, sliding in his embrace, swaying a finger under his nose in the most adorable fashion and looking every bit the cute drunk student with her short wispy hair. "Not another word, Carrero." Finding her amusing, he motioned the locking of a key over his lips and pretended to throw it away before casting her a wink and pulling her back in for another slow groove. Another bout of Emma's terrible balancing act but he didn't care, it was an excuse to hold her a little closer and enjoy how she felt being against him. An excuse to wrap his arms a little tighter and pull her a little more closely than he ever dared when it was just work.

He finally gave up when it became obvious the only way she was going to manage dancing anymore was in his arms this way and he grinned her way. He could take advantage of it or he could do the decent thing and put her down. Grudgingly he chose the decent thing as she always made him feel like he wanted to be better.

Too freaking cute for words. Too goddamn intoxicating.

He tugged her by the hand, watching her unsteady wobble and the way her big eyes watched him adoringly, he had to give her that much. She knew exactly how to wind him around her little finger with just a look whether she meant it or not and he had no will to ever refuse that face. He slid an arm around her shoulders, pulling her close to support her and possibly take advantage of holding her once more. He couldn't help but listen to her drunken rambling with a smile, she was making very little sense, but he just liked the sound of her voice. It was something he never tired of hearing.

She wasn't one of those girls who talked incessantly, in fact, she didn't talk enough if he was being honest. Emma was reserved most of the time, even in conversation and he liked the version that appeared when drunk. That version of her let any damn thing out of her head as soon as it hit her brain and that was a girl he was crazy for, incredibly sweet, a little too adorable and a lot of sexy.

Back at the table, Jake had practically carried Emma with an arm around her waist to the others who were mid-story about a trip they had taken last summer. Jake could hear Hunter reminiscing over the Ibiza party they had thrown for his birthday, that one time they had ended up drunkenly stealing Jet skis and going on a middle of the night adventure while too drunk to be doing anything of the sort.

Jake guided Emma to the group of standing men this time, instead of the seats where Marissa had switched to one directly beside where he had been, sliding a casual arm around her shoulders and pulling her close so she would stay away from that vicious look Marissa had all over her face. Emma didn't seem to notice his over-familiar handling of her, so he took that as encouragement that she was fine with being a little manhandled. He handed her a drink and leaned in to catch up with what his friends were talking about. Leila was on her feet too, standing between the twins, and he couldn't help noticing that Daniel was avoiding looking her way. The boy was completely hopeless when it came to Leila, and he wished he would just sort his act out and tell the girl how he really felt about her.

"Yeah, so Jake's like, I'm sure we can make it ... and he goes speeding off on his fucking jet ski, right in ... doesn't give a fuck." They all burst into laughter and looked toward Jake as Daniel patted his back. Jake was trying to remember the point in the story and mildly aware Marissa was trying to catch his eye again, he ignored her best he could but she was making him uncomfortable with the efforts she was applying and he cast his mind back to that midnight romp in which they managed to get stuck out at sea with a storm brewing and had ended up using a cave for shelter.

"What choice did I have?" Jake cut in, finishing Daniel's memory. "Daniel would have had us sleep out there at that rate, not that he would have minded. Daniel's always trying to get in the sack with me, the boy's still trying to deny his feelings." He joked, taking a swig of his beer and relaxing as he felt Emma's eyes on his profile, looking adoring and kissable as ever. God the urge to just lay claim to her in front of everyone right now was killing him. He wanted her badly and cuddling up together was making things so much worse.

"It's kind of heart-breaking to watch him suffer ... Unrequited love." Richard broke in, stifling a grimace as Daniel slapped his back a tad too aggressively.

"Fuck you. Both of you," Daniel spat a little harshly.

"You know when you know ... Right?" Vincent threw a wink at Daniel and three of the four men burst out laughing, Daniel rolled his eyes and gave them the finger.

"Tried so damn hard to let him down gently, he's just too sensitive." Jake ruffled Daniel's hair.

"I've caught him sobbing into his Haagen-Dazs a few times, when you stood him up, Jakey." Richard shoved Daniel in the ribs playfully and winked Jake's way.

"He stole my *Endless Love* CD when you missed his birthday bash last year. Perfect crying anthems on there for dumped lovers." Leila quipped in throwing a huge smile at Jake and he smiled back, Leila had been trying for months to be okay around Hunter and this trip was the first time in so long they had not tried to kill each another on sight. They had some serious history between them.

"I swear to God, you guys better stop with this shit. Even if I was that way inclined, I wouldn't jump Carrero's bones. I know where he's been, I have standards." All three men looked at Jake with eyebrow wiggles and he only sneered at them. By their standards, his whites were a hell of a lot cleaner, he had at least some morals when it came to the women he pursued in the past.

"Umm, I think I've way higher standards than any of you three." He defended himself with a frown. Suddenly feeling uncomfortable with the topic while Emma was standing so close and almost scrutinizing his profile, he couldn't look her way when talking about past conquests.

God, she had no clue he wasn't even doing that anymore.

"Questionable." Leila threw him a look. He didn't need to see more to know she meant Marissa and almost grimaced at the memory. Everyone could make mistakes, even hellish ones like that. "But you've improved a lot." She then smiled at him concealing nothing. A big hearty, winky type of smile and he felt that hint of warmth knowing she meant Emma. Leila wasn't so dumb after all and maybe it was her he

Carrero Bonus Book 1 ~ Jake's View

should offload to rather than Hunter. Get a female perspective.

"Leave her out of this," Jake warned, squeezing Emma a little more tightly. He may have liked the way Leila was thinking, but he had to make sure none of them got the wrong idea for her sake. He also wasn't exactly too enamored with the way Marissa seemed to be honed right in, staring at them both and giving him her best *fuck-me-now* eyes. He regretted picking a place in her line of sight to stand.

"You know when you know, right?" Vincent smirked Jake's way knowingly, and in that second, he really wanted to throat punch him. Like a performing fucking circus, the other two men joined him in knowing looks and all three winked his way slyly. He glanced to see if Emma noticed anything untoward, but she was busy resting her head into him innocently.

Assholes.

"Daniel certainly seems to think so." Jake made kissing noises at Hunter in a bid to cover the moment of complete awkwardness, letting go of Emma to haul Daniel into a headlock and plaster his cheek with wet, noisy kisses. Fucker could take that for initiating all this in the first place.

"Fuck off, you creep." Daniel fought as everyone laughed. Everyone lightening up from the all too serious turn in conversation much to his relief and he could see even Emma was smiling. Jake came back to put his arm back around her possessively and ignored Marissa once again hitting him with a sexual pout.

Piss off, for the love of God.

"Admit it, you've been planning the Hunter-Carrero wedding since you were just a little girl. It's kind of sweet, really." Jake prodded Daniel with his beer bottle and received two fingers on one hand and one on the other as a response. It was an attempt to keep his focus off what Marissa was now doing with her tongue in the bottle she was holding, he had never had the urge to push it down her throat this badly before.

"You're riding dangerously close to a Hunter free existence. Then we'll see which dude is crying into his Haagen Dazs. We all know that Mr. Smooth Carrero has the biggest man crush on me." Daniel picked up a beer, mock threw his hair back like a woman, and fluttered his eyelashes.

"In your dreams, pretty boy. I'm hoping for a threesome with the twins." Jake winked at Vincent and Richard who threw on matching "EWWWW" faces. Everyone laughed, even Marissa this time which meant she had to stop blowing off the bottle and giving him orgasm looks. He felt that draw for a moment of a guy who definitely had not had enough sex of late and watched for a mere second as she bit on her lip suggestively, memory serving him right about what she used to do with that mouth before sense got the better of him. Emma laying her soft head against his heart almost made him feel guilty even pondering it for a second.

Jake adjusted his hold, so he could pull her closer and rest his arm further around her. She was the only girl who belonged near his heart, whether she wanted it or not. He switched his beer bottle to his left hand, so it hung in front of her and gently took her empty cocktail glass and laid it down, glancing at her happy face for a moment and being reassured that bringing her on this trip was the best thing. He had never seen her so chilled or smiley in all the time he'd known her and even being grossly manhandled by him tonight hadn't brought out one PA telling off. Maybe she was warming to him after all.

Daniel started rehashing another trip last year, another summer vacation a group of them had gone on. There had been sixteen of them that time and of course Marissa, she had tried to get into his bed on more than one occasion, and he had even woken up with her writhing on top of him naked, trying to get him hard. He had considered it for all of ten seconds before shoving her ungracefully to the floor and then proceeded to fuck every girl she'd brought with her over that next couple of days just to piss her off.

Marissa looked his way devilishly, obviously remembering his little backlash, and he felt smug for a moment. He maybe had no feelings for the girl anymore but getting some sick payback for what she had done to him always got a reaction. They seemed to keep doing this; going around in circles year after year until he had met Emma ... Now it no longer interested him at all and he had no intentions of trying to beat her at any more games of seduction ever again.

The waitress came with a tray and laid another round of drinks on the canopied table. Jake handed Emma a fresh cocktail with his free hand, his mouth lingering close to her temple a little longer than necessary as he smelled her, weird and probably a tad obsessive but she always smelled edible. Tropical fruits and slightly sexual in a way and he liked to just do it because he was fucking weird when it came to her. He had long ago stopped even questioning the shit he did around her.

Hunter started eyeing him oddly, waving his phone around and talking about some vague memory that Jake could barely remember. He was flicking his phone at Jake enough that he finally took the hint, letting go of Emma and leaning in to see. He was being strangely secretive by only showing it to Jake and then he saw why.

There was no picture only the start of a text which read.

Jake ... She seems totally into you tonight ... Fucking get in there ... Look at her man, she's all over you.

Jake looked at Daniel with a warning frown but couldn't help but feel a little torn. Emma had been cuddling up to him as much as he was since standing here, all the flirting on the dance floor with him and now glaring Marissa down; he was starting to wonder if he should make a play for her or not.

He didn't know if it was the alcohol or what, but Emma was different on this trip, had been since they arrived and maybe he should stop acting like a woman and just go for it. Daniel was obviously seeing something he wasn't.

He caught Marissa once again giving him the bedroom eyes and sighed internally. Staring at her for a moment to give her the back-off warning, he felt Emma looking his way.

God, she looked beautiful with that hair.

He couldn't help that same rush of lust whenever he looked at her and being drunk was certainly not helping at all, he pulled her in instinctively for a kiss, part of him saying DO IT and then chickened out and hit her on the cheek platonically instead. She was making him all kinds of nervous now that he was even considering trying to make a move on her tonight. He wasn't sure whether to listen to Hunter or not, he had zero clues when it came to Emma. Still no way closer to ever reading her but Leila's encouraging smiles his way and now Hunter giving him a green light had his palms getting clammy and his throat drying up.

Fuck ... He was scared shitless.

"You're very quiet ... Want to go back to the boat?" he said to her softly, hoping that maybe if he got her alone he would relax and be able to read her signals a little better. Decide if she wanted this or not. Decide what to do instead of freaking out like an amateur over here.

"Yes, please, I'm so tired, it's been a long day." She smiled at him and his crotch most definitely stirred, Emma's husky tone was a little too inviting for platonic thoughts.

Fuck, maybe Hunter was right, Emma was definitely looking at him in a way he had never seen her look.

"Ooh, party on the boat." Leila chanted and jumped up, impressively bouncing her boobs, all male eyes immediately followed because that's what men were designed to do, seek out impressive tits when jiggling. Even Leila's, even though Jake realized how weird that was and felt a harsh dig to his ribs. Looking down he could see one very unimpressed look from Emma. He knew this look. Her haughty little PA glare which signaled she was not happy with him, a little hint of jealousy from his green-eyed princess. Feeling suddenly euphoric that she had just given him the green light he had been looking for, he gave her an apologetic shrug and wink.

Baby, tonight you're going to be kissed senseless.

* * *

Going back to the boat Jake had been disappointed to find the entire party followed them, so they had no time alone. The boat ride back had been eye-opening though, with Emma standing between his legs as he had perched on the edge of the side and her arms around his neck. She had been about an inch from his face the whole time talking about nothing specific, her eyes had kept moving to Jake's mouth longingly and he had to curb kissing her about a thousand times even though his hands were on her hips and she was pulled practically into his groin.

One little inch forward and a tiny head tilt was all it would have taken, she was already mirroring his pose and

Jake & Emma

screaming "kiss me". He didn't know if she had any idea what signals she was giving him right now or if she was subtly telling him to go for it, she was obviously drunk and feeling more carefree and it just confused him as to what to do. She was giggling enough, touching him enough, and if she had been any other girl, he would have high-fived himself as all the cues were there that he had scored. But this was her, and she was innocent in all ways sexual, she trusted him, and he didn't want to kiss her in front of these people, anyway. If and when he did make a move he wanted it private, so she could relax and decide without pressure if she wanted it. He didn't want to ruin anything between them and that kiss so long ago in the hotel had made him wary of trying too haphazardly.

On the boat, he had left her to wander the deck with Leila and headed to the lounger, he was going to let her make the moves if that's what she wanted. Let her relax, let her come to him and play it by ear. It was the only way he could think of playing this where she was concerned and that way he couldn't screw this all up by assuming it's what she wanted.

He kicked back and decided to let it go a little, drink more and get as merry as her if he was going to stop overthinking all of this. Maybe that was half his problem, he was trying to stay sober so he wouldn't make moves on her when he should really be throwing caution to the wind and going with the flow. That's what she seemed to be doing tonight and watching her dance, drink, and get in the party mood was definitely doing it for him.

"You're in there, you know?" Daniel slid down on the lounger next to him and smiled his way, waving a bottle toward Emma and Leila on deck. "She's been giving you the come on since she got to the restaurant, man, what are you waiting for?"

"You don't know her like I do … She's nothing like the women we normally chase, Danny, she requires a little gentle handling." Jake frowned his way and then back at Emma. She was laughing with Leila and falling over one another while trying to change the song on the stereo. He smiled at just how adorable she was.

"Is this what love does to you? Makes you wimp out and over cautious. The normal Jake Carrero would have had that chick naked in less than three minutes, fucked, and back on deck to party within the first couple of hours on this boat. Man, by now you would have fucked her a dozen times in every position and moved onto someone else … You really are pussy whipped." Daniel slumped back and shook his head at Jake, smirking uncontrollably.

"Shut up … I don't want to be that guy anymore." Jake mirrored Daniel's pose and slid another beer from the table to cradle on his abdomen. Both staring up at the perfect starry sky contemplating things in general.

"No, you don't want to be that way while your head is all invested in her. If she was out of the picture, you would revert to kind, mate." Daniel prodded him in the shoulder and he flicked him away.

"Maybe she made me realize that doing all the shit I've done in my past isn't enough, it was fun, but it was never fulfilling enough to make me happy. It's why I hit it so hard and so constantly … Looking for more and never finding it … Until her." Jake looked towards his best friend with a sigh. Daniel regarded him coolly.

"Look, she's obviously hot for you tonight so go for it, do me a favor though. If she doesn't want more when you're both sober, Jake, then you need to move on, get back in the saddle and put this shit to bed. Bang her, spend the night making her fantasies come true but know if a line is drawn then all of this stops. You go back to who you were, and you let that chick do her job." Daniel's stern tone was not that of a guy being a dick, but a best mate offering wisdom.

Jake had to agree with what he was saying despite it not being what he wanted to hear. Tonight, was the turning point. If he made moves, and she wanted it, then he would go for it, but if she didn't then he would stop it all. And by *all,* he meant all of this celibate shit and pining for her and accepting it was never going to happen. None of this was healthy, and he had no more energy for it.

"I should stop! I think I've had enough." He could hear her protesting Leila's advances with more alcohol. Voices coming their way and Daniel raised an eyebrow at him before sliding off to join the twins dancing badly on deck with Marissa and Miracle.

"Hush now, we're on vacation … party, party, party!" Leila was loud and obnoxious like her normally drunken ass could be.

"End up comatose or throwing up in my own shoes, you mean?" Emma sighed as he watched her grabbing the rail for support. That perfect little body encased in that short floaty red dress and looking a little too divine.

"Your loss, sweet cheeks." Leila pouted cheekily and turned toward the dancing group with a smile, swinging her hips and leaving Emma to either follow or not. Emma turned his way looking at him in a way he knew meant she wanted to be beside him right now.

She wants this … Take her cue, Jake.

"Come, *bambino*!" Jake's eyes met hers, a look between them that he couldn't mistake. Years of those same looks from women meant that, even on her, he could recognize it. Emma most definitely was finding him attractive enough tonight to want something more than just platonic touches and with a little beckoning finger wiggle, he patted the lounger beside him suggestively.

She wants you, she wants this! Relax and go with it.

His heart had upped its beat and his body was definitely feeling a little clammy, nerves kicking in and telling him he should drink a hell of a lot more. Jake never got nervous around women … Ever.

She pushed herself off the rail without hesitation and with a sultry look pasted on her face, chewing her lip, she made her way toward him on unsteady legs. She got within a foot of the bed and fell ungraciously on top of him. Luckily even drunk Jake had fighters' reflexes and caught her soundly. Okay, maybe in some awkward places that his hands shouldn't have strayed, but he pulled her to the side of him and wrapped an arm around her quickly to avoid drawing attention to the hand that had fully palmed her breast.

She has amazing tits.

"Crap." She breathed through a giggle that made him only want to pull her closer, her skin was a little cool from standing up on the deck all night and he wrapped his warmer body around her to cocoon her in his own heat.

"Bit drunk there, Miss Anderson?" He laughed at her, enamored by that twinkling set of eyes and the precious smile stuck in place. Trying to erase the feel of her breast from his hand.

"Of course not," she slurred and then looked immediately confused.

Jake just cuddled her more, too goddamn perfect for words. He had it bad, and he knew it. Everything she did had him weak for her and even something as simple as cute slurring of words had him wanting to squeeze the life out of her.

"Glad to see you letting go." He smiled, almost nose to nose with her.

"I think falling on top of your boss is more than letting go." She laughed, relaxing in his arms and regaining control of her vocabulary once more.

"I'm not your boss for the next two weeks." He winked suggestively, plying on the hints thickly that he was completely on board with however she wanted to play this. Full flirt mode coming out but being played low.

"Okay, I shall rephrase … Falling on top of your temporary, not boss, is overdoing it." She giggled again, the breeze blowing her hair up around her face suddenly, and he reached out to smooth it back so he could continue to stare into those cool blue pools of perfection. Her eyes had always drawn him, from that first time in his office those baby blues had captured him and haunted his mind, always. She could unravel him with one look.

"Do you need me to put you to bed?" he asked, hoping that if he got her away from watchful eyes and maybe alone they could further explore what this was tonight. He also hoped she was picking up the subtle hints in that question.

Gentle handling, Carrero. Listen to her, read her signs.

"Do I not need to put *you* to bed?" she slurred again, and he couldn't help but laugh at that suggestion.

If only.

"I'm sure I can handle way more alcohol than you, tiny." He joked, keeping a firm hold on that body and letting his hands trail down her back slowly toward her ass, she wasn't stopping him, anyway. All signs that he wasn't reading this wrong at all.

"I'm not so sure, I haven't seen you walk yet." She pointed at him in the universal drunk air jab. Too goddamn adorable for words and her mouth was most definitely getting closer to his, her body moving toward him so very slowly.

"I'm sure after seeing you make an attempt at that, it proves you're worse than me." He shifted to move his groin away from her a little, she was getting too close for comfort, and unlike most women who liked to feel the effect they were having on him he knew Emma wouldn't. She wasn't like any girl he had ever known, and this game of seduction was nothing like any he played. The ball was in her court, and he was just playing along with whatever she was allowing. He wouldn't scare her off by moving in all Carrero panther-like.

"I like your dimples when you smile." She prodded his face. Focusing on his features a little too closely, distracted by them it seemed and licking her lips as her eyes moved to his mouth. He all but groaned.

She's giving every prompt and signal unknowingly, innocently … Fuck.

"And there she is." He grinned trying to deflect just how horny she was making him right now.

"There who is?" she asked in confusion, a frown creasing her forehead and eyes coming back to his.

"Drunk Emma … How are you doing? I missed you, baby." He smiled, although truth be told she had been drunk since the restaurant.

"You missed drunken Emma?" she asked, blinking suspiciously.

"I did." He smirked as that little jealous twinkle hit her

Jake & Emma

eyes. All good signs for him.

"Why? … Do you like her more than me?" She pouted with sad eyes, not even smiling when he laughed at her and shook his head. Too sweet for words.

"You are drunken Emma …" He soothed, shifting his knee between them a little to keep that wriggling body of hers from getting back into his groin as that was the way she was heading. Aware of it or not she had inched herself right against his chest and abdomen and caught her feet in his, she was trying to get as close as possible and it was taking all his willpower not to flip her on her back and just stick his tongue in her mouth. He was almost certain she wouldn't refuse it right about now but the voices of the others on deck were killing this. He wanted it a little more special than making out in front of them, especially Marissa and her wolfish eyes that had been undressing him all night.

"No. I'm not … I'm just Emma … Drunken Emma is …" She looked flustered and he could only laugh. "Why are you laughing? I'm being serious!" She pulled her hands across her chest between them defiantly, but it only made her more appealing, he prodded her nose playfully.

"Both Emmas are you, they just choose to come out at different times. You're cute when you pout." He prodded her in the face lightly again before pinching her nose. He could touch her all day and never tire of it.

"Why do you like her more?" She slapped his hand away sulkily, more pouting and the saddest eyes he had ever seen, it just made him want to laugh all the more.

God … adorable personified. Jesus.

"How can you not love this version of you?" He wrapped his arms tighter around her, now that she had taken them from her chest, back to her previous close position and planted a kiss on her cheek. He snuggled his head into the crook of her neck and maneuvered her body to mold into his a little better. If he wasn't in direct line of that luscious mouth, then he would less likely pounce on her and down here he could at least inhale that sweet skin and perfume to his heart's content.

Jeez, she felt good.

"Pffft … I don't love her then." She tried to wriggle free huffily, and he had to lift his head just to see that wounded expression which was all but killing him, she really had no clue how freaking awesome she was.

"Because I do?" He smiled at that adorable frown.

"Yes!"

"That makes no sense." He jested, stopping the urge to poke her in the face. Playground flirting techniques were not normally his thing, but she seemed to bring it out in him.

"Yes, it does … If you like her so much, she must be a leggy bimbo." She sulked and looked away from him, all hints of childish green-eyed monster on show.

Interesting.

"I already told you, I don't actually like leggy bimbos, Emma." He lifted his head more to stare at her fully nose to nose. He instantly thought about stopping that sad little face with a kiss, he was close enough, sure enough, that she wanted him to, and yet he didn't want to do it this way. Not here. He inched close enough, eyes fully locked on the target and didn't take the shot.

What the fuck is wrong with you?

"I don't believe you." She almost gulped at the slight reaction to his near kiss, another hint that she was into this. He just had to stop being a pansy and just do it. Stop worrying about fucking things up and kiss her. He had built this moment up in his head so much that now he had too many nerves to try. She couldn't throw any more signals at him if she tried.

"Well, that's your prerogative." He smiled softly this time, willing himself to just go for it. Moving in slowly once more, pushing his crazy scared shitless self aside and just forcing himself to kiss her.

The scrapes and shifting noises on deck snapped his attention guiltily away as though his mom had just walked in and caught him trying to fuck someone in his room and he looked toward them. It was obvious by the way Daniel was maneuvering Miracle's dress off that sexy time was about to get underway and Daniel wasn't exactly shy about fucking in front of others or letting them join in.

Shit.

"Time for bed ... I know what Daniel's like. Show-time equals go time!" He didn't like the fact that Hunter was doing this with Emma here, he would never expose her to that sort of degrading show. Emma wasn't that kind of girl.

"What's he like? What do you mean 'show-time'?" She looked at him questioningly as he effortlessly pulled up with her in his arms, he was getting her below deck before she saw anything that made her uncomfortable.

"He likes kinky sex, he's an exhibitionist, doesn't matter if you're male or female, he'll try to pull you in, he has no qualms about fucking in front of an audience." He frowned Daniel's way knowing no way in hell would he ever let any of them touch his girl.

Jake caught sight of Leila getting up to leave too, she had never been into that whole scene and well, being Hunter, she didn't want to hang around to see. Richard was following her.

"Will you join in?" Emma squeaked at him, a completely crestfallen look on her face thinking that he might want to. His heart warming a little at the obvious upset thinking he might. He had her.

Fuck no … She was far more alluring than that shit.

"No, it's not my thing, Emma." Not anymore, not in a long time and especially not when he had something better to be a different guy for.

"You said you did it on your dad's boat when you were younger … group … stuff." She accused him softly, obviously thinking back to old conversations from when he was stupid enough to think they would just stay friends. He regretted being so open about his past, wondering if it made her look at him in the way she was looking at Daniel right now. Disgusted.

Fuck.

"Who do you think was at the root of that?" He raised an eyebrow toward Daniel accusingly, not that it was fair, he had never forced him into all that just helped it along. He pulled Emma along by the hand and toward the stair to the lower deck trying to get her away from this quickly. The music was louder now and Miracle, already lying naked on a lounger, had started to touch herself. The girl seriously had no shame, and it made Jake grimace. Why he'd ever thought that lifestyle was better than this was beyond him. Looking at Emma he knew he would never go back to that shit even if he never got with her.

"So, you liked it then?" she asked looking back once more as Marissa got up and began a slow strip tease, her eyes following them. Jake ignored her and shrugged. Putting an arm around Emma to guide her and hold her up on those Bambi drunk legs of hers.

"I was young, it's just sex. I was pretty much partying and pissing my dad off at every turn." He tried to play it off casually, wishing he had never let her know what was going on and just whisked her off quickly. She was too inquisitive when drunk and this was not putting him in a good light at all. She stumbled on the carpeted floor and he righted her, pulling her close protectively. He could feel the effects of the alcohol more now that he was upright and the relaxed feeling moving over him fast. At least it was quelling his nerves.

"You don't do group sex anymore?" She hiccupped, still chasing this goddamn infernal subject and he could only frown and sigh internally.

Jesus, Emma. Are you trying to ruin my chances with this?

He smiled at her in complete frustration with her line of questioning, looking skywards for a little help. She was like a dog with a bone on this and it was killing him.

"I like your smile." She smiled, obviously instantly distracted in her drunken haze.

"No, I don't, and I like that you like my smile, shorty." He stopped and pushed her against the wall to steady her as he pulled his phone from his pocket as soon as he felt it vibrate, he swiped the screen seeing Daniel's text on the front and had to hide a visual reaction.

Fuck her hard so she never wants to go back to being mates … Good luck!

He wanted to kill him about now, swiping the screen closed and shoving it back in his pocket.

"I like when you laugh like that." He glanced up at her trying like hell to stop visualizing fucking her now, thanks to Hunter, and trying instead to focus on her sweet girly giggling instead.

Carrero Bonus Book 1 ~ Jake's View

Focus on her sweetness, not her cleavage, not her mouth, Carrero.

"Like what?" she asked innocently, still unable to stop grinning. He regarded her for a second then realized he had pretty much pinned her to the wall so every inch of her was against every inch of him, the hardness growing down between them in his pants was becoming a little too prominent and he shifted away.

"Unguarded ... I like drunk Emma." He pulled her off the wall and lead her to her room, he would take her there and give her one last attempt at turning him down before he would make a move. As long as all the signs were the same as the last hour then he was going to kiss her. More if she wanted but right now he just wanted to kiss her more than anything. Sex would be a bonus he wasn't counting on.

"I like drunk Emma too," she sighed, following him as he opened the hall door, his hand still grasping hers gently.

"I thought you said you didn't?" He frowned at her with a confused smile. Her drunkenness was as polar opposite to PA Emma as she could get.

"I was jealous ... You like her way too much." She pouted and looked a little forlorn which made him laugh out loud. Leading her the short distance to the next door.

"You're the same, Emma ... No reason to be jealous, *bambino.*" He calmed his laughing, opening her bedroom door into the dark room and pulled her to the base of her bed, he had deliberately put her in a room next to his so he could be close if she needed him.

Letting her go, he sat her on the end of the bed and undid her high-heeled silver sandals, sliding warm hands over delicate feet on his knees and feeling her watching him. He knew he should switch the lights on, but he knew what he was doing in here. He was going to relax her, then he was going to move in without hesitation and go for it. No lights needed for that.

"Nooo, you like one more than the other." She sighed. He smiled and shifted closer, so he was between her open naked legs with her dress sliding up high as she accommodated his body, nose to nose almost and practically the same height with her sat on the low bed and him on his knees. Not physically touching but he could feel that sizzle of electricity between them sparking in the darkness. He had been right about her giving off signals. He had no doubts anymore and this last little invited maneuver was sealing the deal. PA Emma would never have let him slide into her open legs so suggestively.

He reached out, touching her hair and running a hand through its silky softness, watching in the dim moonlit dark for her reactions. As expected she tilted her head toward his hand and parted her lips suggestively, her knees pressing to either side of his thighs as her body instinctively responded to him. All the things he had been watching for.

Maybe sex was an option after all.

"I like both versions of you in different ways, equally." He sighed, trying to keep his libido under control as his blood started warming up at her obvious come-ons, keeping close.

"What do you mean 'different ways'?" She blinked up at him innocently. He sighed, running a hand across her face lightly and moving her hair to tuck behind her ear, he chewed his lip as he tried to think of the most diplomatic way of answering her. Truth be told he was in love with every version of her, but drunk Emma let him in more than the others, he got a chance of more with her. That's the only reason he wanted more of this version.

"PA Emma is cool and capable and she's the best

assistant I've ever had, she's funny and sharp, and she's good at what she does. I like PA Emma." He nodded to himself, rattling off his mental tick list. Finished with her shoes, he kneeled up, so even though he was still on the floor his head was towering over Emma and his groin was not so pelvis to pelvis.

"You like her in an employee, employer way?" She reached up and toyed with his spiky hair childishly, instantly making him smile and raised eyebrows at this innocent un-Emma maneuver. Alcohol was definitely bringing out a whole new side to her and a flicker of guilt hit him in the stomach all of a sudden.

Kissing her like this would overstep the mark; she trusted him to take care of her when she was drunk, and all of this was just drunk Emma letting go a little. The flirting, the come-ons ... She wouldn't be like that sober and he was realizing how much of an abuse of her trust it would be to kiss her like this. It hit him suddenly and seemed to swamp his intentions with doubt at an alarming rate.

"Yes and no ... I just like her, because she's her." His eyes came to rest on hers, an overwhelming feeling of disappointment hitting him in the gut.

He couldn't hurt the relationship they had this way.

"And drunk Emma?"

"I'm a little infatuated with drunk Emma if I'm being honest." He pulled her hand down and straightened up to leave, resigned to doing the decent thing and walk the fuck away. Taking every ounce of his inner strength to do this.

"You are? Why?" She sounded sulky, maybe sensing a change in him but he had to do this for her. She meant more than a one-night stand or awkward drunken kiss and the more he thought about it, the more he knew he couldn't do this. Daniel was right, his head was fucked when it came to her and he over thought every single detail.

"Because she's fun … she doesn't guard what she says … or does." He nodded toward her fingers, reinforcing what he was saying. Sober Emma would never have played with his hair. "She giggles and lets her hair down."

And trusted him to not take advantage when she was vulnerable.
Shit.

"So do most of your leggy boobs." She sulked at him again, big doe eyes that sucker punched him more, and a little petted mouth that was killing him right now. He couldn't believe he was contemplating walking back to his room and stopping this.

"They're not the same. Not even close, *bella.* They don't have the other side to her … That's what I mean by "I like you both". One can't exist without the other. I wouldn't like there to be only one and not the other." He shrugged being almost completely open about his feelings for her.

"So, you like my split personality? … A lover of the cray cray." She grinned playfully motioning in circles at her temples and crossing her eyes. He smiled, that overwhelming affection for her cuteness hitting him hard and making his mind up for him. He wouldn't abuse her trust when she was drunk. He loved her and that meant no breaking boundaries when she was vulnerable.

Fuck you, Carrero, wimp!

He moved another hair from her face taking a last longing look with the intention of saying goodnight. Every part of his body was yelling at him, but he didn't care. He wanted her to be able to face him in the morning and deep down he knew this was not the way it should be between them.

"It's not split though, there're glimpses of both versions all the time, just one chooses to dominate ... I see drunk Emma sometimes in PA Emma. When she occasionally relaxes too." He had lost all his merriness, sobering up hard and lingering when he should have been walking out.

"Maybe she doesn't know how to relax all the time," she confessed with a conspiratorial wink. Emma couldn't look anything but gorgeous to him.

"I think she's scared," he answered thoughtfully, not sure if it was her he was talking about anymore, or him.

Was he too scared to try to move things on? Was her being drunk an excuse?

"Why?" She watched him carefully, that sweet inquisitive expression on that flawless face. He stood up, his hands moving to cross across his chest and moved away from her. Putting distance between them deliberately.

"Because letting her guard down means she lets go a bit of control and she likes to hold it all together. Letting go makes her vulnerable, leaves her exposed, and that's worse than death for her." His voice was steady and low, betraying none of his emotion; it's what he knew about her, but she didn't know it was about him too. Moving in on Emma was letting his guard down fully, removing the final barrier which had kept him safe from complete devastation. Wimping out was about protecting him as much as her. Protecting his heart from being broken again.

"If I'm vulnerable, people can hurt me ... Men can hurt me," she whispered into the darkness of the room, sounding suddenly fearful, bringing him out of his own head and that fierce protective instinct for her coming out to play. Watching her he bent so his forehead met hers and pressed their noses together, an awkward position for him but as

Jake & Emma

natural as breathing. He wanted to comfort her and make her feel safe. He would always keep her safe. It took precedence over everything.

"I'd never let anyone hurt you, Emma." He breathed against her. His hands coming down to hold his weight on the mattress at either side of her thighs so he could stay leaning over her. Bringing them close enough to breathe the same air and smell her gentle tropical skin.

"What if you couldn't stop them?" She suddenly sounded so young and vulnerable and he wanted to squeeze her badly. He would die to protect her, always.

"I'd always stop them." He promised with conviction in his voice because he truly meant it. Emma sank toward him impulsively, looking like a lost child, reaching up so she could wrap her arms around his neck and brought their foreheads to touch. He wanted to close his eyes at the way she initiated this cuddle and imprint it to memory, she didn't often initiate touch at all.

"You won't always be around," she said quietly.

"I'm always around if you haven't noticed," he said softly, bringing attention to the fact that since he had met her he had engineered almost a constant presence on purpose. Even before he knew what she was becoming to him, he had wanted her around him all the time.

He felt her lift her head and tug him a little closer, so their eyes could lock. The most intimate thing Emma had ever done, and he had to steel himself back in to stop the impulse to kiss her again. She looked so trusting which only calmed his fire.

"I guess," she whispered at him.

"Let go, Emma ... trust me to look after you ... if not long-term, then for these two weeks at least. Trust me to protect you." He was almost begging her. He wouldn't do this drunk but if she was this way tomorrow, then maybe he would. Sober, he would kiss her if she let him.

"I'll try," she whispered, not loosening her hold on him at all.

"Good girl." His arms came around her, pulling her up to him slightly for a gentle embrace to say goodnight and leave before he did anything stupid, lifting her from the bed for a full body embrace.

"Don't say that to me." She paused mid hold, causing him to halt. Her voice childish.

"Why?" He was suddenly confused at what he had said.

Good girl? What was wrong with that?

"Just don't …" she said a little more firmly, he smiled in acknowledgment and slowly pulled her the rest of the way to cuddle her. Dismissing it for a conversation when she was more lucid. Emma snuggled into him a little too readily, making his body react in the worst kind of way for this given situation; he had to release his hold or impale her. The sudden release of her body made her stumble awkwardly and Jake cursed himself internally, reaching to catch her and losing his own footing as his toes hit the bed leg painfully.

Fuck. Graceful this was not.

He leaned forward too far to try to keep hold of her and somehow completely lost his balance, too drunk for these kinds of maneuvers and even though she weighed practically nothing he went down on top of her, nose to nose and laughing like fools at the awkwardness of their ungraceful collapse. His face was so close to hers and his body fully connected in such an intimate pose that for just a second, he couldn't react, his mind a whirling mess of '*kiss her … don't kiss her*'. He just stared instead like a dumb asshole and couldn't foresee Emma lunging at him full force in a flash.

Her mouth connected with his so suddenly that she almost winded him and took a millisecond to realize that she was kissing him, Emma was kissing him!

Fuuuuuckkk.

His heart somersaulted to his abdomen and sent all manner of craziness inside of him. His mouth and hers entwined in seconds, moving into the one thing he had wanted for so long and being hit with an overwhelming onslaught of emotions and sensations all at once. Euphoric tingles and extreme hunger, losing himself in her taste.

Goddamn, she tasted like peaches and cream and her soft lips and softer tongue were made for devouring.

She kissed like an angel, a little unsure at first, obviously inexperienced which only made him want her more. He knew he should stop it, but he couldn't. The second her lips had met his he was lost to her and no amount of willpower would drag them apart right now. He was adjusting his body to lean all over her without crushing her and losing himself into the kiss in ways he had never experienced.

This was love, he couldn't deny it anymore. The way she felt, what kissing her made him feel. He was lost with no hope of a comeback after this.

His hands moved to her hair and around her throat impulsively, wanting to hold her to him and claim her. Softly holding her still so he could lead the kiss, showing her how to mold to him as she found her way. Her movements became more confident and meeting him flawlessly, he loved the fact that it was obvious she hadn't done a whole lot of kissing this way, her inexperience was noticeable, but she was adjusting herself instinctively to him. She was his perfect pure angel.

God, she was made to kiss him.

He could feel her heart rate increasing under him, her body moving to accommodate him more comfortably and her breathing getting shallower as she got more turned on. Jake knew without a doubt this was heading for sex and he knew he might not have the willpower to stop it, lust consuming him and love driving him.

He caught her hands in his and pressed them against the mattress beside her head, pulling away to catch his breath momentarily, trying to slow things down and gain control. Trying to rationalize this, but he couldn't, the way she was looking at him just pulled him back down. He had no control over this, she had opened a flood gate, and he wanted her so badly he had no say anymore. His head was blanking his thoughts out and just lost to the sensations.

He dropped back to that inviting mouth and gave himself all in, no regrets, no holding back, just kissing her more passionately and harder. Both breathing hard and fast, Emma responded with fervor, arms wriggling to be free to go to him. Legs moving up around his waist and inching herself against his abdomen even though he was trying to keep distance down there. She was moving against his body suggestively in time to the kissing and making him groan wildly. He knew Emma was no virgin, she had mentioned boyfriends from her teens, but she clearly had never been a casual sex kind of person which made this all the more intoxicating for him. Her movements were not skilled and honed, there was an innocence and almost awkwardness, holding onto him as though asking him to guide her. He had been with enough women in his lifetime to know this was almost as close to her being a virgin as he could get, and he fell in love with her all the harder.

She wouldn't go all in for just a drunken night surely?

He pulled away and kissed her again, this time sucking

Jake & Emma

her bottom lip seductively and testing how far she may want to go. She writhed under him, reaching up to try to kiss him again, her body fully molded to his and despite his obvious arousal she wasn't backing down but pressing herself to him. Jake's head was cloudy with lust and he could no longer think straight, nothing except getting her body naked and being inside her.

She was clinging to him and trying to pull him further into her, moaning at his touch, moaning as his tongue moved back into her mouth slowly and she began scrambling her hands free to haul him down by the shoulders greedily as though pinned together was not close enough. There was no denying she wanted this as much as him and he was beyond stopping it, his hands moving to skim the side of her breast and reveling in how fucking sexy her body was to him. Holding his weight up so he could shift against her harder. Bringing his groin to her pelvis and parting her legs further so there was no denying where he was pushing this, she just opened up and let them connect. Her body heat, scorching hot in the apex of her thighs, fueling his desire.

He groaned against her mouth, her body too perfect for words, hand moving down to trace her thigh and head toward her heat ready to take this a step further without hesitation. That point of no return.

There was a massive bang in the hall behind them, he had left the door wide open and the sudden noise made him jerk around quickly, shielding her to protect her from whatever it was. There was lots of hysterical screaming as the door filled with a dark looming figure of a man and Jake pulled away from her reluctantly to turn and look. Confusion clearing his foggy brain.

"What the f—?" Jake was shocked yet angry that he had finally got to this point with the girl of his dreams and some asshole was wading in to ruin it. He was still on top of her, braced on his arms but their bodies still entangled achingly.

"Jake? Jake?" The voice at the door sounded hysterical. He recognized Richard's voice instantly.

"What is it?" he snapped, raging that this was his fucking life right about now.

"It's Daniel, he fell off the boat … We can't find him."

The Carrero Effect
~ The Holiday: Part 2 ~

Jake was searching under the water, too dark to see anything and scrambling with his hands at anything that felt like it could be Daniel. Panic gripping his stomach as he frantically surfaced for air and dove again. He had hit the water without a thought the second he knew Danny was in here. No cares that he was maybe too drunk for this and just endlessly searching despite his muscles aching and being so heavy he could barely move anymore. It felt like it had been hours instead of minutes and he still hadn't found him. He wouldn't give up on him, he wouldn't lose his best friend this way.

Surfacing for air quicker this time he took a moment to drag more into his burning lungs and wipe the water from his eyes. He could hear yelling from the deck, crying from Leila and other voices but he was fully zoned-in on the surface of the water looking for any signs of him.

"He's here, Mr. Carrero," yelled out one of the crew from the speed boat nearby and he felt his body lose all fatigue and started swimming their way frantically. He could see them hauling a lifeless body into the boat under the moonlight and a sickness swept through him, a fear that maybe they had been too late which only made him swim faster to his friend's side

* * *

The hospital had given Jake some dry clothes to wear, he hadn't really thought about anything when he had jumped into the air rescue chopper holding Hunter's hand, only that he had to be with him at all costs. It had all passed in a blur of drama and chaos. Daniel's lifeless, pale face lying still and closed-up on the stretcher below him, he felt like he had barely breathed in that entire journey to the mainland hospital.

Hunter had been breathing on his own but still wasn't conscious and the paramedics had been messing with tubes and ventilators while Jake curbed his panic the best he could. He had lost a friend this way once before, saved them from drowning only to have them die later from too much fluid intake.

It had felt like an eternity sitting in that hall waiting for word, his stomach churning itself in knots and his hands trembling and cold when they had got here. The ship's captain had been sent back to the boat as daylight had broken. He wanted him to take care of Emma in his absence, it was the only rational thought he could formulate, focusing on her to give him some peace.

He hadn't given himself much chance to think about what had been happening with her when Daniel had fallen overboard, he had been focused on him and what was going on, the fear and agony of searching for Hunter. Anytime she had come into his head he had pushed her back down, wanting to analyze it later, not tarnish the happiest moment of his life with possibly the worst. Until he knew Hunter was going to be okay, all thoughts were on him. Losing Danny would be like losing Arrick, he was as close as a brother and would never forgive himself if he died.

"Mr. Carrero? Mr. Hunter is asking for you." A young female voice drew his attention, looking up at a young nurse in blue scrubs beckoning him to follow, so he did without hesitation. She smiled his way warmly.

"He's okay? He's going to be okay, I mean?" He tripped over his words, half relief and half exhaustion. Walking behind her and trying to drag his heavy weight with him. He felt about a hundred years older suddenly.

"Yes, he will be kept in for observation of course but he's fine. His father has been notified and on his way."

Jake sighed, relief washing over him and a sudden ache to wrap arms around Emma shocked him. He didn't have his cell with him to call her. He'd gotten here in soaked clothes, a shirt, and chinos, not even wearing shoes.

Jake was ushered into a side room that resembled every hospital he had ever been in, a lot like that time he had gone with Emma to Chicago. A single bed that was tilted into a comfier position, surrounded by white curtains and a bunch of machines and Hunter sitting grinning at him from the middle of it all like a fucking asshole. Dressed in a hospital gown and tucked in like a goddamn child under blue sheets and a blanket.

"Dickhead," Jake grunted at him but still moved in for a shoulder to shoulder man-hug and patted his best friend on the back with sheer relief.

"You're my hero, baby, hear you swam your little lungs out like Aqua Man trying to find me." Daniel winked at him, but he had the urge to just punch him in the face for being so fucking normal.

"Fuck head. At least pretend to be remorseful or at least injured, right now you're making me want to hurt you and I wouldn't feel any guilt at all." Jake flicked Hunter in the forehead in agitation then hauled a seat over and slumped down ungraciously.

"Charming! You look like crap … Tired and definitely not like a guy who got laid." Hunter eyed him up warily and Jake only stuck the V up at him.

"Yeah, well, whose fault is that?" he growled at him grumpily, rubbing his face and feeling several layers of fatigue hitting him all at once. Relief was a funny thing, it let loose everything he had been holding back for hours and all of a sudden, he was drained in the worst kind of ways.

Goddammit, he was beyond tired and no longer anywhere near drunk at all.

"Sorry, bud … So, how far did you get with little miss icy pants?" Hunter grinned but Jake only glared at him coldly.

"Don't call her that. Danny? How the fuck did you fall off the boat? There are safety rails for that specific reason and even a drunk asshole like you couldn't just tumble over them." Jake shifted in his chair trying to find a comfier spot but couldn't. His body aching and desperately in need of sleep.

"Misdirection! Interesting … So maybe started something but didn't finish it huh?" Daniel smirked his way and got another finger aimed his way.

"How?" Jake repeated.

"Okay, I'll go first if you go second … no bullshit from either of us … deal?" Hunter looked sheepish and peaked

Jake's attention. He obviously had something juicy he was hiding. He sighed and then nodded knowing Hunter wouldn't give this topic up.

"I saw Richie trying to coerce Leila into my wild little party, pulling at her dress and trying to haul her back … She was saying no, and I just saw red. I flew for him but being drunk as fuck I misaimed and went straight over the rails. I don't think they were even looking my way so everyone thought I'd just jumped up and Superman dove into the ocean." Hunter shrugged, a little color rising up his cheeks with embarrassment and Jake couldn't do anything but burst out laughing. He leaned into his knees and just gave in to the worst kind of hysterics.

Relief, pent-up emotional trauma. Who knew? But he laughed so much his sides started to ache, and tears poured down his face, when he stopped he realized Hunter was laughing too. Just how ridiculously close he had been to death in trying to save Leila from an orgy he had started. The whole thing was completely crazy.

"Jesus, Danny … for the love of God please tell the fucking girl you love her for fuck's sake!" Jake hauled his arms around his ribs to stop the ache, but Hunter just raised a knowing eyebrow at him. They knew it wasn't that simple.

"Touche!" He winked at Jake but was met with another heavy sigh.

"Yeah, whatever." Jake shrugged and once again pushed thoughts of Emma away, he didn't really want to think about this right now.

"So?" Hunter pushed at him with a finger and Jake glared back. Telling him was inevitable and a part of him wanted to talk about it. Let it out of his head.

"We kissed … for a while … would have been more if

some idiot hadn't nosedived off the fucking boat." Jake shrugged and tried to relax but talking about this had him tense and edgy. He couldn't pinpoint why. It had been everything he had thought it could be, more, but now in harsh daylight and sober as hell he was worried as to what would happen now. How Emma would feel. Maybe not getting to sex had been a saving grace instead of a calamity.

"You don't think she wants more do you?" Hunter was eyeing him up intensely, reading his best mate effortlessly as he always did.

"No." Jake hated to admit it, saying it out loud hurt like hell but something deep down was telling him he was crazy to think someone like her would even want more with someone like him. His past, his lifestyle, and all the shit he had done even while she was his PA. He had fucked it all up by not realizing from day one he should have been showing her he could be a guy worth more. Not a playboy asshole with a string of fuck buddies and a long history of wild parties and reckless acts. It was no wonder Emma never looked beyond friendship, the chemistry was there for both of them, but he was an asshole to let her see into all that he had been so easily. Last night had been drunken fun for her, he was stupid not to realize that.

How could he win over a girl like her, a pure and sweet angelic girl when he had done nothing to deserve her?

"Look, man, you know how I feel about this … If you think there's no future in it you need to be the one to cut ties." Hunter was frowning at him and he knew what he meant. Firing Emma so they didn't work together anymore was the last thing he would ever do. He couldn't imagine not having her in his life.

"I can't … I won't," he said firmly, his no-nonsense tone that even Hunter knew not to argue with.

Jake & Emma

"Then you need to cut ties emotionally. If she wants to be just friends and co-workers, then you need to get up and go back to who you were until she doesn't mean anything anymore." Hunter was watching him, laying back on the cushions a little helplessly.

"Has that worked for you?" He regarded him thoughtfully.

"It helps. Over time, I hope I feel nothing for her, but over the last couple years I find it easier to put her out of my head." Hunter shrugged again, and they both looked up at the ceiling to contemplate the craziness that was Hunter's love for Leila. Jake tried to imagine doing the same thing and couldn't. He was far worse than Hunter in terms of how he felt and his relationship with Emma wasn't exactly something he could just drop and run off to the other side of the world from. He was her boss and love aside, he did actually need her at work. She was amazing at what she did, and he didn't have the heart to look for another PA. He didn't want another PA.

Jake got back to the boat in the early morning, a long drive from a passing farmer he managed to flag down and then having to persuade a boat trip out to the moored yacht from a local when he got to port. Not having his phone or any form of money on him had been brutal, but he was glad to be finally climbing the silver ladder onto the back deck of the boat. Hunter was being kept in for forty-eight hours to make sure he would have no lasting effects and some minor antibiotics to make sure he didn't catch any bugs. He would come back to the boat in due time, so Jake was happy to leave him. Seeing one of the crew approaching at his arrival he beckoned him over.

"Go to my room and get some money from the vanity and pay the guy for the ride … Just take whatever's there."

He patted the crewman on the back knowing he was trustworthy and left him to speak the native tongue of the local to pay him for the kindness. Jake was too tired to deal with any more, he wanted to find Emma and check she was okay, tell her that he was back and then go to bed. He was exhausted and almost dead on his feet.

"Ricardo?" He turned to the young man quickly "Where is Miss Anderson?" he asked pointedly.

"Up on deck, sir, she was on the loungers about five minutes ago." The young man nodded his way, receiving a pat on the shoulder as way of thanks and Jake headed for the stairs to the upper deck. It was early even for an early riser like Emma, suggesting she had probably waited on him all night and that didn't make him happy at all. She would be as tired as him.

"Emma?" he called out as he got to the top of the deck and could see her laid out on the double lounger like an angel resting on the clouds. God, she was a sight for sore eyes, and just being back within ten feet of her relaxed every taut muscle in his body. He felt like he had been tense waiting to get back to her and could finally breathe now that he could see her.

"Hey." She smiled shyly from her position on the lounger as he walked forward intently, she just looked too inviting to not go to her and all thoughts of anything else swam from his fuzzy head. She was like a constant lure for him, pushing sense aside. He slid down beside her on the lounger with a satisfied sigh, his body giving way to the comfort of lying down. He sprawled alongside her, not caring if he draped all over her, too fatigued to move, and lay on his front. He buried his face in his arms to block out the light and felt like he could fall asleep instantly beside her, the smell of her and her nearness was like being home, and now his brain was shutting down with relief.

Despite his brain closing down slowly, he could feel her breath on his arm and her eyes on his profile, silently looking at him. He could sense her, her shyness at saying anything vibrating his way and as much as he wanted to just sleep he wanted her to be okay about last night too.

"I'm still awake," he mumbled, sliding an arm out across her waist with his eyes closed, pulling her to his side so he could snuggle into her and kill this insane need to stare at her. He wanted to know what she was thinking, but he didn't have the energy to do anything about it. He moved his face nearer her neck so he could tuck his forehead against her hair and inhale all the sexy goodness and subtle tropical scent that was just her. He had missed her like crazy.

"You smell good," he muttered almost incoherently, still with eyes shut and sleep trying to overtake him. He could feel her slowly beginning to tense her body, her breathing becoming shallower and the tell-tale signs of Emma going into PA mode, all business and no emotion.

Fuck, he didn't need this version right now.

"Thanks," she muttered a little tightly. Jake sighed internally that she wasn't even going to give him five minutes to rejoice in last night before ripping this to shreds for him. He smiled against her naked skin with a little hint of defeat, smiled because he knew her only too well.

"Are you ever going to just learn to let go, Miss Anderson? When you're sober." He sighed again, wishing she was still drunk for at least a little while.

"What do you mean?" She sounded irritated, maybe a little surprised.

"I can feel you … stiffer than a board … why so formal after last night?" He smiled again. Teasing her might be more fun than an argument right about now, not that he could do much. He had no use of his limbs anymore. He felt her movements and the tell-tale motion of her twisting her hair anxiously, her cute little annoying habit of nerves on show.

Goddammit, Emma.

He reached up, covered her hand in his and pulled her fingers away from that soft, beautiful hair.

"Relax, I only want to sleep," he mumbled, returning his arm to its previous throw across her waist casually. "Stop thinking and sleep with me … you look tired." He commanded a little more than he meant to, but he wanted this last time with her before reality set in and she found every reason to rip his heart out. He felt her eyes on his face again and knew she was probably glaring at him for pulling her fingers out of her hair like she always did. Truly a return to her uptight former self and not even a hint of carefree holiday Emma left on show.

"I'm not tired," she huffed childishly, feathers ruffled for whatever reason and whatever he had done this time. Hungover, Emma was on show and even though it was normally cute, not so much today when he actually cared about what had happened between them last night. He felt her slide out of his arms, leaving him feeling a little empty.

"I'm going for a swim," she added as she rose, voice all cool and very PA and Jake could only sigh at her return. Last night had obviously pushed her further than she was comfortable with and here she was reeling it back in again with a vengeance. Jake lifted his head to look at her walking away, sexy and cute all rolled into one perfect little package of sheer angelic beauty. He felt that ache of longing at knowing this would never be what he wanted, and she was already closing down on him.

"Don't drown … I don't have the energy for a repeat of last night." He sighed, watching her leave with a serious bout of regret at leaving last night, as much as he was glad to stay by his best mate's side he couldn't help but wish he had stayed with her and seen through whatever last night had been. More now than ever seeing as cold and closed off Emma had made a grand return. She was back in work mode, and he was not too happy about that at all.

When Emma had left the deck Jake hauled himself up, the lounger no longer appealing without her on it and dragged himself back to the confines of his own room to sleep in peace away from the death rays of the sun.

Leaving it dark and only kicking the door semi-closed he collapsed face down on the bed, barely managing to haul the covers back with his heavy fatigued body and passed out immediately.

* * *

Jake finally woke up feeling almost normal, his room was still in darkness, and he had no clue how many hours he'd been asleep. He was still in the exact position he'd flopped down in and was now stiff as hell.

He pulled himself up and dragged his aching muscles to the en suite shower in an attempt to wake up fully. He hated sleeping the day away even if he had an excuse and wanted to make sure he did something more active than lazing around today to counterbalance his messed up sleeping pattern.

Once showered and dressed he headed up on deck to see what the crew had going for breakfast, or lunch, or whatever the hell time of the day it was. For all he knew it could be evening, anyway.

Heading up into the sun he was surprised, and a little irritated, to see Emma had fallen asleep under the highest point of it in the day, it was noon judging by its position, and she was only being saved from the rays by a book over her face.

He knew it was her just from that little body alone, she had a figure the other girls should envy, soft curves and perfectly proportioned little limbs. Even her dainty feet always fascinated him. He'd never been a fan of small delicate girls before Emma but somehow it only added to everything about her that was perfect.

He sat down on the lounger beside her, smiling at the romance book cover with a shake of his head. The girl was complicated, to say the least, he would never have pegged her for romance books, and he slid it away slowly to reveal her peaceful perfection underneath.

Tiny little nose and perfectly kissable lips, a perfect face if he ever saw one and the tiniest hints of freckles forming over the bridge of her nose now she was getting a tan. He gently brushed her hair away from her forehead, savoring the silent moments before she woke up fully. Taking in a face that would haunt him for a lifetime.

"Hey." He sounded husky as she began to rouse with the sun fully hitting her face, adorably sleepy and those perfect soft blues that he loved so much flickering open to melt his heart some more.

I love you, bambino.

"Hey." She half smiled, half blinked up at him sleepily, his heart aching a little too much.

"You shouldn't sleep in the sun," he scolded gently, watching her trying to focus on him. Even though he'd put himself in between the sun and her to shield her, she seemed to be having a hard time looking at him properly, squinting at the brightness.

"I didn't intend to." She blinked some more as Jake slid his sunglasses onto her face, smiling back when she smiled at him in that endearing way she had. He knew they had to talk about last night and set things straight, not just brush it aside as she seemed to want to do. He didn't want to do it here either.

"Want to go somewhere?" Jake looked off to the ocean, away from her face. A deep sense of trepidation that this was not going to go how he wanted it to but that doing it was unavoidable.

"Such as?" She sounded inquisitive, mellower than before he had gone to bed and less PA toned.

He shrugged in reply, he just wanted them away from here, away from the others who would start questioning him about Hunter, tilting his head up to watch the sea crashing on the distant shore to give him some sense of calm.

"Anywhere but here." He sighed dejectedly. He had told Hunter that deep down he knew Emma didn't want a relationship with him, but he had always held a tiny spark of hope that he was wrong. Being here now with her after last night and how normal she seemed had killed all his chances. He knew undeniably that Emma was never going to see him as anything other than a boss and a friend.

"How's Hunter?" she asked gently, watching his face a little too closely.

"He's fine … he will be. They just need to monitor him. Secondary drowning is a risk when you swallow as much as he did." He answered on autopilot, his head too wrapped up in what was missing between them to divulge much about

Danny.

"Secondary drowning?" she asked looking at him shyly.

"You can drown long after you come out of the water. It's in your lungs still." He tensed, remembering Blake Carlisle, his childhood friend who'd drowned after a stupid drunken boat party. It hurt to remember him.

"So where will we go?" she asked a little more brightly, a smile plastered on her face, but it did nothing for his mood. She was so far removed from the Emma of last night it was scary.

"We could drive somewhere." He went back to watching the horizon instead of that beautiful face of hers, tense, distracted. He just needed to get things moving and get this over and done with. He had formulated a plan at the hospital last night with Hunter. A way out of this emotional mess he was in if things were looking hopeless with her.

"Okay." She smiled a little warily, unsure of his mood. "Shall I get changed?"

He shook his head, looking over her floaty dress and sandals, she was always gorgeous no matter what she chose to wear but in the summer clothes and dresses she was even more so.

"No ... You look perfect." His eyes flickered down the length of her as she got up, waving her book at him to say she was going to put it in her room. He watched her walk away elegantly and felt his stomach drop heavily. He had got enough from these few minutes to know he might be putting his plan into action later today. Emma wasn't the same girl of yesterday, the connection was gone, and she was most likely never to get that drunk again, knowing how far they had gone.

Minutes later, Emma walked back on deck toward him, looking every bit the angel who held all the keys to his heart and every bit the destroyer of it. He smiled, despite feeling like absolute hell, and gestured for her to follow him to the stairs again to get off the boat.

* * *

Driving the coastal roads on the cliffs above where the yacht was moored in the rented sports car wasn't helping Jake's mood much, despite the companionable silence between them, he was tense as hell. He caught her looking his way a few times, but he ignored it, keeping his eyes on the winding road, and handling the powerful car expertly. He had been using the quiet time to think things through, look for ways to fix this, other outcomes and yet always came back to the same problem. Emma just didn't feel the same way about him, and he had to accept it. Sighing to himself for the hundredth time, he tried to focus on just the here and now, of being with her and enjoying the beautiful scenery and the rest of their trip.

Feeling her eyes on him once more he tried to lighten his mood, smiling her way softly, remembering a little too well what she had felt like in his arms. That soft mouth and smooth skin, that tongue of hers meeting with his, that body molded so seamlessly to his own. If anything, he could imprint all of it to memory for a lifetime and never regret one second of it. To be able to kiss her so freely had been more than he had ever imagined it could be.

"So? Are we literally just driving then?" she asked brightly, breaking the silence between them and looking his way openly, a small subtle smile on show.

"Nope," he replied unemotionally and just kept his gaze fixed on the crazy road to maneuver another dangerous narrow turn.

"No clues?" She tried again with another look his way, a small hint at irritation.

"None!" Jake just answered in the same unemotional one-word way. He didn't much feel like talking just yet, he had a scenic destination they were heading for that he could stop at.

"How do you know I'll like it?" She bit a little more aggressively, temper rising quickly in her. Emma was obviously still hungover and easily irritated but it only grated on his already fragile mood.

He shrugged as a response.

"It's not fun is it?" he responded dryly, unable to keep a curb on the emotions building up inside of him now that they were nearing the lookout point where he intended to stop. His own hangover biting and emotions fragile.

"What?" she snapped back around, catching his face turned her way for a second, both of their eyes narrowed at each another.

"Being closed out." He tried for nonchalant, but emotion betrayed his words, he just sounded sarcastic and he knew he was being an asshole, but he couldn't help it. Getting closer to stopping and really talking was no doubt getting closer to Emma telling him this would always be a boss and PA relationship and he was hurting like hell. "What does it take, Emma?" He asked impulsively, really wanting to know what he had to do to just get her to look at him the way he looked at her.

He shifted gear, eyes back on the road and whole body tense as hell while he waited on her response, he was driving a little faster and heart beating louder. He knew he was working himself up into this frenzy of a bad mood and had little control over it.

"Jake, please … what are you talking about?" Emma

shifted awkwardly in her seat, fixing her seat belt as though the speed was making her nervous and he eased his foot on the gas a little. Slowing down to round another turn.

"You're not even going to mention last night? Is that another conversation over?" he snapped at her as emotion overtook and regretted it almost immediately.

Cool the fuck down, Carrero.

"You didn't mention it either." She spat a little too aggressively back at him. Riled by his mood, obviously and changing the whole tone of how he had intended this conversation to go.

"I was waiting to see if you would." He tried to keep control of his tone this time, trying to defuse the anger and just talk. He wasn't doing a good job of it at all and every word out of his mouth sounded snarky as fuck.

"Why?" she snapped, still pissed, and he could only shrug. He had wanted her to broach the subject, acknowledge last night in some way because it fucking hurt him that she hadn't. That it had been nothing to her except a drunken mistake.

"Jake, it shouldn't have happened, we crossed a line." She glanced his way, softening her tone the way she did at work when she was trying to soothe a bad mood over some shitty business meeting. She was pandering to him, and he couldn't fucking stand it over this. He lost the last ounces of control on his temper.

"And there she is! Right back to square one." The sarcasm was thick in his tone. His body stiffening in his seat with sheer anger and heartbreak fighting each another for control.

"What's that supposed to mean?" She turned at him angrily.

"Anytime you get close, Emma, even a hint of letting go, you snap right back in and shut the door. No conversation, no acknowledgment of it, just wham. Over!" He barked at her, letting his anger loose, unable to stop the infernal ache in his gut from leaking out.

"What?" She hissed with a sardonic laugh. "Because I won't sleep with my boss? I'm not letting myself go? That's being closed off?" She turned away anger flaming her face, body seething rage, and he wanted to punch the goddamn windscreen so badly.

"I don't think there was any doubt about it last night. It's not the issue … it's the afterwards, Emma." His voice was laced with venom, anger seething from every pore, his body tense. He had never been on this side of it before, women had always wanted more from him, and he hadn't felt anything. Knowing that was now Emma's stance got to him more than anything ever had in his life, knowing what she was probably thinking right now because he had been that same cold bastard so many times.

"I was drunk … being stupid, anyone can make a mistake!" She huffed and stayed looking away from him. Shifting herself away so she could turn her body from him toward the door. Jake felt that surge of complete ache hit him hard, rage kicking in and he slammed the car to a halt with his foot hitting the floor on the brake pedal. Uncontainable pain oozing from every pore.

This wasn't her … his Emma was not this cold-hearted, unfeeling bitch who just slammed sex like that; who dismissed last night as a drunken mistake not worth mentioning.

Everything loose in the car flew around them dramatically but he didn't care, he needed to get out and away from her before he ripped the goddamn steering wheel off and used it to smash the windscreen out.

He felt her looking his way as he hauled off his belt and got out of the car. Stalking far away from it and leaving the door wide open, walking to the cliff edge to try to regain some control over the huge swarm of painful emotions consuming him right now. For a second, he had an urge to jump off the fucking cliff just so it would stop. He dragged in a few deep breaths to cool his jets, simmer his mood until he had control once more.

His pain dulled down as sheer anger overtook him, anger that she would be this way about last night. Anger that despite knowing it would turn out this way, he had still gone down this fucking route. Anger that he hadn't just left it alone and enjoyed a day on the beach with her doing anything except this shit. He was a fucking moron.

Calmer, he turned back and slid into the car once more, swallowing it down, breathing hard.

He knew there was no way of coming out of this conversation now and he had to do this, for his own sanity if nothing more. Things between them couldn't keep going on this way and last night had been a final line for him. He couldn't stay loving a girl who only wanted friendship.

"It's not about sex, Emma," he said quietly putting his hands back on the steering wheel to give him a point of focus, but he didn't start the car. "It's about this eternal need in you to stay in full control. Never letting anyone in, never letting yourself enjoy anything and letting your guard down." It was about her inability to love him the way he loved her and as much as he tried to skirt around the issue, there was no getting away from it anymore. It was make or break time.

"That's not true," she replied defensively, looking at him like a wounded rabbit caught in headlights. His gut aching again that he was doing this to her right now.

"Really? Emma, I've been with you for months now, I've seen just about every version of you there is … Tired, grumpy, bossy, happy, PMSing like fuck." He was calmer, her sad expression simmering the heat of his temper, but his voice was strained, that edge to his tone that hinted at anger bristling below the surface.

"I've seen vulnerable only briefly." He glanced at her and she looked away a little too quickly. "I get it, Emma … you're strong, you want everyone to see that. You don't need anyone, but it's not who you are … and it's not true."

He didn't want it to be true, he wanted her to need him.

"Yes, it is. Do you ever think that maybe you overthink it and try to see stuff that isn't there?" she spat angrily, turning to him frostily and glaring him down in that way she intimidated people at work. He didn't even blink at it, he knew this look on her was nothing more than a defense mechanism to make people back off.

"I think I know you better than most people." He sighed, knowing this was going nowhere that he wanted it too. He did know her, knew that he was fighting a losing battle and he no longer knew why he was even trying.

"What if I don't know how else to be, Jake?" She turned to him accusingly "You keep pushing … keep telling me to let go but what if I can't? What if this is me … this is all I know … I'm not capable of doing it any other way because I don't know how." She started yelling at him, eyes brimming with emotion and he couldn't help but ache. Even mad she was too beautiful for words, mad and closing him down little by little. All he was ever going to get was last night, the memory of a kiss that he wanted one more time.

Throwing caution to the wind and knowing this would

Jake & Emma

probably make her madder than hell he thought "fuck it" and threw his lips against hers. Without hesitation, his mouth molded to hers and lips searched hungrily for the feeling of completion she gave him. He was surprised when she responded to his kiss and opened her mouth to meet his. Jake felt every part of him sag into her, his hands finding their own way into that soft hair, tangling his fingers, and pulling that sweet mouth closer. Tongues gliding against one another, lips perfectly connected and the easy motion of two people so right to kiss each another that it made him die a little inside. He felt her fingers travel up his chest and tangle in his shirt collar, tugging him toward her and his heart soared.

Maybe he had been wrong about this and she was finally letting go.

Tilting her head more to accommodate his mouth on hers, giving as much to him as he was to her, not breaking the embrace but pushing it higher and hotter. Breathing heavily and getting lost in the sensation of the kiss equally. They both moaned lightly as the kiss deepened, soft lips and intense feeling pushing him on.

He wanted her closer, needed to feel that body he longed for against him. Letting go with one hand and sliding down to find her belt buckle he unclipped it. Sliding an arm around her waist he pulled her into his body as best he could in the small confines of the car, pressing as much as he could have her to him hungrily. Praying for seconds longer to enjoy this but feeling her start to lose the passion between them. Her hands loosened their hold on his shirt, her kissing keeping time with his, but he could feel her reluctantly pulling back as her palms turned to his chest and she gently started pushing him away. Disappointment, anger, heartbreak all colliding at once as he reluctantly pulled away from her and sat back, letting her go dramatically, no longer able to keep his emotions in check. He looked at her with such devastation.

"That's exactly what I mean!" he bit in pain. "This is your biggest enemy, Emma … not me." He tapped her temple with a finger, an extreme crushing pain in his chest as he watched her soft expression move back to cold defensive PA mode, back behind her safe barriers.

"Why did you do that?" she spat at him, both breathing hard and trying to regain composure.

"To prove a point," he snarled and turned away. He had no point to prove, just a longing to kiss her one more time and feel everything he had felt once more to savor it because deep down he knew it would be the last fucking time. This was over.

"What point?" she asked him accusingly, anger and emotion all over that face. So confused. He scrubbed his hands through his ruffled hair and sighed, grasping at some sense of control and thinking he should just have got out and gone for a walk, but he didn't.

"What does it matter?" his voice was deflated. He was deflated and tired. He was giving up and just wanted to go back to the boat and forget this day ever started.

"Fuck you!" Emma screeched at him angrily, tears filling her eyes and shocking all the anger out of him. She had never actually sworn at him while yelling like that, and he was rendered momentarily speechless.

He hadn't ever seen Emma scream at him quite like that either, complete emotional rage. She turned, shoving the car door open, and was gone in a flash, storming away from the car. Impulsively, he followed in hot pursuit. Guilt eating at him and an inability to ever just let her be upset, even if he was the cause.

Fuck, fuck, fuck.

Jake & Emma

He caught up in seconds as she stalked toward the road, pulling her back into him and spinning her around to face him, tear-stained and all and it just hit him in the stomach like a punch. Emma crying was something he could never handle, she rarely did it, and when she did, he felt like the biggest dickhead on the planet. He hated seeing her cry, it wounded him in ways he could never explain.

She tried to fight him off angrily sobbing, but he just folded her into his embrace, pushing his face into her hair and cradling her so she couldn't get away, trying to soothe her.

"I'm sorry … Emma, stop … Emma. I'm sorry." His voice was raw and strained. She kept fighting but was losing against his sheer size and strength, she was no match. He just held her close, stopping her outbursts and trying to cuddle her in until she finally began to slump and give up the effort. Finally stilling in his arms, silently crying against him yet not really cuddling him back. He knew if he let her go she would still walk off.

"I don't want to fight with you." His voice was quieter, closer to her ear, his crazy mood taking a new direction again and just trying to stop the stupidity between them. No matter how he felt for her, above all she was meant to be his friend and friends didn't hurt each other like this.

"I don't want to fight either." She swallowed a sob. Slumping into him dejectedly and he could only hold her closer, that horrid feeling of sadness sweeping through him once more.

"Maybe we should go back to the boat." He sounded tired, he was emotionally exhausted and physically fatigued from the events of the last twelve hours. He had no fight left in him and right now all he wanted to do was lie down and try to block all of this out of his head for a few hours.

"Maybe," she whispered with slight relief and Jake just snapped at her easy agreement. Losing his temper erratically for no obvious reason other than all of this just fucking sucked and he wanted her to care more about it. He couldn't explain or control any of this anymore.

"No," he snapped, surprising her and making her tense in his arms, looking up with a look of pure confusion.

Fuck this shit … Fuck her and everything she did to him!

He stalked to the car quelling the urge to push her away from him, placing his hands on the hood in a bid to stop the angry energy surging through his entire body. He needed to go to a gym and beat another boxing bag to death to get rid of it this time. Glaring at the hood of the car and wondering how much damage he could inflict before his hands gave out.

"I can't do this, Emma," he snapped, his gaze was steady on the hood of the low sleek car. He clenched a fist and went for a punch, stopping it millimeters from the hood and laying his palm back flat on the hot sun heated surface. Deep breathing to try to curb every internal crazy impulse.

"Do what?" Emma tried softly, keeping her distance and obviously a little wary of his mood. He tried to quell it some more for her sake.

"This! Us!" He waved his hand in an exasperated motion, turning back to her, looking at her with sheer frustration and frowned.

"You drive me crazy … and not in a good way." He sighed. Facing the car again. His body emanating all kinds of crazy signals no doubt, but he had no control over all the crazy messed up emotions colliding from months of this hell with her.

"I do?" Her small fragile voice sounded completely surprised. She had no clue at all the effect she had on him which only strengthened the fact she saw only friendship between them. She was so innocent and naïve to what this really was for him.

Too angelic for words.

He sighed again, and his face tensed.

"You frustrate me on so many levels." He carried on, deflated again. Just so fed up with everything that this was.

"Sorry," she murmured sarcastically, he could tell she was probably rolling her eyes too, while he wanted to just forget he ever met her. He threw her an unamused look over his shoulder, seeing her look down to twiddle her fingers nervously and it only made him sigh. Looking back at the car to get a grip on himself and reality, he began kicking at the solid rubber of the tire with his boot toe childishly, trying to just distract his head from the urge to throw something. He needed to self-calm.

"Why do you never talk about your childhood?" His tone softened, new direction, trying to change this whole topic to something else … anything. He didn't even know why he would choose this topic among them all. He just needed to talk about anything else, maybe a little insight into her past would help him understand why she was this way. Simmer his anger.

"What?" He heard the defensive scared tone in her voice instantly and it didn't help with his own mood. "There's nothing to talk about … You have knowledge of the highlights," she said drily, that warning tone in her voice she used when the conversation was over.

"I know bits and pieces, Emma, mostly from getting you drunk." He glared at her accusingly, so pissed at everything right now, even though he was trying to dampen it. Especially this one-sided fucking relationship they had and the fact that after everything, she couldn't even let him know the details of her past. It said a lot about how she felt about him.

"Where is this going?" Emma glared back at him suspiciously, always closing him out. He was sick of being shut out.

"It hurt you?" His eyes came to rest on her, trying to push every ounce of aggression away again with a mammoth effort and barely holding on. She messed him up in so many ways, and she just had no clue at all.

She looked away, crossing her arms around her body protectively and he just sighed and crumbled inside. He was mad, he wanted to be mad but somehow all she ever did was make him feel guilty and want to stop being angry with her. No wonder he was all over the place. He had no control over his own emotions.

"It's the past and it should stay there." Her voice wobbled a little this time with raw pain, and she moved away to turn her back on him. Jake took that hint of softness as a signal that maybe this wasn't the brick wall he was meeting this time after all.

"Your mom? You don't talk about her much either." He pushed, his voice gentler, trying hard to just not be a dickhead. Coaxing her to open up about this gave him a little hope that he meant something to her at least. This topic was easier than the previous one and it was something he had always wanted to know. It was distracting him from his anger, which was a good thing.

"She's my mom … What else is there to say?" She replied coldly, still keeping her back to him defiantly.

"Tell me about her." He turned on the hood of the car and sat down to watch her, intrigued that for once he wasn't having to battle any information out of her and it was helping take his mind off other matters. Her poise was hostile and stiff, but she hadn't ended the conversation and closed up in true PA fashion like normal.

"My mom is a sucker for a sob story." Her voice was raspy with emotion yet held a hint of anger, at him or her mother he wasn't sure. He hated knowing that she had never had the childhood she deserved, hated knowing she had been hurt in ways that someone like her should have never endured. "That's about all there is to her."

"She has bad taste in men?" He got up silently and moved toward her, aching to soothe her while she talked about this stuff, just wanting to be there for her. Despite everything, all Jake ever wanted was to help her and learn more about what made her tick. She walked further off, putting the distance back between them a little as though she had sensed him getting closer, always holding him at bay.

"That's an understatement," she snapped angrily.

"They hurt you?" He had moved faster, got to right beside her before he had spoken again. Instinctively reaching out to her like he always did when she was close, the smell of her shampoo in the fresh air luring him against her, his fingers moving into her hair near her ear. Flexing his fingers into her scalp, causing her to lean into his touch, with a sigh and dampening over his mood like a balm. Touching her always brought him calmness, even when the topic was hard to digest. She leaned into him and he was lost to her almost instantly. His other hand sliding over her shoulder on the other side and sliding down her arm a little. Savoring the softness of her creamy skin with little resistance.

She always feels so fucking good.

Leaning in close to the back of her head, breathing slowly

Carrero Bonus Book 1 ~ Jake's View

and placing his mouth on the back of her hair, inhaling her, and curbing the urge to kiss her pain away.

"Some ... Some just wanted to ..." Her voice weakened as she swallowed hard. His hand left her arm, snaked around her waist, and pulled her into his body smoothly. His mouth moving to her neck gently and pulling her tight and close to him to be the strength she needed.

"She didn't protect you," he whispered against her collar bone, the soft delicate smell of her skin bringing him a sense of completeness, the gentle soft curves of her body making the pain in his chest fade a little and he just held her, wanting to always keep her safe. He could stay this way forever.

"She did what she could," she mumbled, softly allowing her body to meet his, having a little too much of an effect on his ability to think clearly and instinct at being joined with her was taking control. He couldn't stop his nose skimming her shoulder and neck, the hand that was in her hair trailing down her naked arm and wrist and back up. He couldn't deny that no matter what he would always want her this way, always want to touch her and devour every inch of her. Even while trying to give her solace about that bitch mother of hers a part of him wanted to turn her in his arms and just kiss the pain away, lose himself in that mouth and against that honey-sweet tongue.

"She didn't stop bringing men around her child, *miele*." His voice was hoarse with a mix of emotion and lust, and he felt her tense again, this time he knew it was at his words not his actions, his mind coming back to what he said and honing in on a tiny glimpse of Emma's past.

"Why did you leave Chicago ... Leave her?" His hands were still trailing down her arms and up again, but his focus was fully on her words now, the thought that his Emma had run from home to find safety in New York of all places. The thought of the girl he knew running scared from anything made him feel sick to his stomach.

"I needed to walk away from all of it … I needed to save myself because no one else was going to." Her voice broke a little, and he knew without turning her there were more tears and it tore him open to the bone.

"I think you need to talk to someone about all of this, Emma … a counselor … I could …"

She jerked away instantly, spinning to glare at him angrily. All moods snapped closed with simple words, and suddenly she was fire and anger and squaring up to him like he was the enemy.

"Not a goddamn chance," she spat, all venom and pain in her face. "I'm not fucking crazy!"

"Emma, that isn't what I said," Jake responded a little surprised at her sudden turnaround in mood, seeing a side of her she normally kept so under control. Sheer emotion and rage seeping from that beautiful face. He attempted to put his arms around her gently again, but she held out a hand stopping him. He stayed back, allowing her breathing space to vent. Unsure how to deal with the fire he had always sensed was just under the surface.

"Don't okay … you wanted to know … now you know, and that's the end of it." The strength was back in her voice, PA Emma had returned, and she stalked past him toward the car, keeping her eyes averted. Her whole demeanor closing up, standing taller and her grace and mannerisms of the polished PA sliding in defensively. He could read her signs, she was putting that fucking wall back up because he was an idiot that somehow always pushed it. He was pissed as hell again, instant anger flooding back too, but mostly at himself.

"Don't do that," he snapped accusingly, following her

back to the car, close on her heels, he grabbed her arm to turn her, but she yanked it away.

"Do what?" she yelled, deliberately looking anywhere but him in an attempt to get away. He grabbed her arm again and tugged her around to face him harshly, this time succeeding.

"Don't shut me out again, clamp down like you always do. Not after everything, I'm … I'm sick to death of this never-ending fucking circle." He raged losing his temper at always feeling like he would get so far and then boom, door slammed shut in his face again, driving him crazy.

"I didn't want to tell you; You just keep pushing." She wrenched her arm away, chin lifting defiantly. "Let's go back to the boat. I'm hungry and I'm tired." She sounded so cool and closed off he could feel himself erupting again internally.

Always the goddamn same shit with her.

He lifted his hands to grab at mid-air in sheer agitation, not sure if he could choke her about now and gritted his teeth, eyes burning, he paced away from her again, cursing and raging into the open air. She ignored him, turning and getting back into the car. Jake walked to the car and got in, slamming his door, and buckling up in complete stony-faced silence.

He knew when something was futile, he knew when to give up and stop going around in circles of fury and rage that would only end with him doing something stupid as hell. Jake had a lot of flaws but his worse was his impulsive knee-jerk reaction to any kind of hurt. He knew he could be a massive jackass when feelings were involved, and he was done with this once and for all.

"Conversation fucking over," he muttered to himself, starting the car and throwing it into gear as he pulled back out onto the road, he turned the car and headed back to where they had come from; breakneck speed to expel some of the energy building up inside of him wanting to blow out like an explosion. He needed to just get her back to the boat, dump her on deck and put some much-needed distance between them.

He turned the stereo up loud indicating he wouldn't attempt conversation, in fact, he had nothing left to say to her. She was just messing with his head in all kinds of ways, and he couldn't do this anymore. Noticing her hand in her hair twisting it anxiously he lost what hold he had left of his temper. Seeing her like that always irritated him, but now it just fucking enraged him. He tugged her hand out of her hair aggressively.

"Stop fucking doing that!" he barked over the music, eyes glinting at her with fury. She glared back haughtily.

"That hurt," she snapped, reaching out to turn the music down, he had no idea what was even playing it was all just noise to drown her out, and it was failing. She touched her head at the root of the hair she had been twisting indicating he had pulled it and he felt bad despite his anger. He always felt stupidly guilty when it came to her. She had a way of making him feel like the biggest asshole on the planet effortlessly. Maybe being an asshole was what he should be doing and kill this once and for all. If they weren't friends, maybe they could just be professional and not give a fuck about each other anymore.

"I didn't mean to hurt you," he apologized through gritted teeth. "I'm sorry." He meant it, but it sounded like it lacked conviction. He was done with all of this and he just had to get her back to the boat and out of his face for a while so he could think.

"I don't know why it bothers you so much," she spat at

Carrero Bonus Book 1 ~ Jake's View

him. "I don't know I'm doing it." Angry flashing eyes aimed his way once again, and he literally wanted to just hit something.

"It bothers me because it's a sign that you're anxious, that you're nervous or upset ... I don't like it," he snapped back, sick of feeling like this all the goddamn time, sick of feeling like he should walk on fucking eggshells around her.

"Oh, so you want me to unleash vulnerable Emma, but only if she doesn't act nervous or anxious ... Makes so much sense." She seethed. He glared at her, his jaw tensing, fire meeting fire. The sizzle of electric between them causing the air to crackle. He looked away and focused on the road, gripping the wheel hard in an effort to not slam something with his fist. She brought out so much rage in him with so little effort.

He got them back to the port in record time and didn't bother to get out when they pulled up, waiting for her to open her own goddamn door and go first so he could take a minute to hang back. He took a moment to calm down and was glad to see the speedboat was still moored to the jetty, he wouldn't have to wait around for the ship's crew coming for them; guessing the captain was still in town after bringing them over here, and he would send the boat back for him later, he had Jake's number.

Going back across the water to the boat was silent, and she kept herself standing away from him, gripping the rail and looking out to sea. He wasn't going to try anymore, he had made up his mind that enough was enough, and he was ruining everything by being fucking hung up on her. He had to remind himself that she wasn't anything more special than a million other girls out there. He just needed to get her out of his head, and he could only do that with some real time apart. Maybe that was the issue, too much time spent

Jake & Emma

together every goddamn day had made it impossible to ever really move on.

When they moored to the back of the yacht, Emma didn't wait for him, just hopped up and off the boat and headed up to the top deck. Jake handed off the rope to the crewman who appeared to greet them.

"Someone will need to go back for Max later, call him and tell him I brought the boat back," Jake said abruptly and left the young man to secure the boat before following Emma upstairs.

When he got up on deck, Emma was already at the buffet making a food plate, her back to him and he seriously felt like yanking her around and just choking her. She had him so wound up and pissed that he couldn't think straight. No woman, except maybe Marissa, had ever caused this amount of a reaction in him and he needed to be far away right now.

"Oh, the love birds have returned," Leila squealed and threw herself around Emma for a hug, she grinned Jake's way, but he only glared back.

"We went for a drive." Jake glared at anyone who dared to look his way then turned on his heel and headed back to his room. He wasn't staying here for this crap feeling like this. He needed head space and time out. Heading back down to the lower floor he pulled out his phone to text Daniel.

You may be right about putting my Plan B into action. J

He got to his room just as Hunter replied, he had his phone sent over to him with belongings first thing this morning before heading out with Emma to make his stay in hospital more comfortable.

Sorry to hear it, man, but onwards and upwards … Fuck her out of your system.

Jake stared at the screen for a moment before sighing in resignation.

I intend to. See you in a few days. J

Jake stormed to his room and kicked the door shut with a professional kick-boxing maneuver, every nerve ending tingling with the need to release some pent-up tension. Jake was a simple creature, he expelled his excess energy in four ways. Either through fighting, sports, other extreme physical pursuits or sex. And lately, sex had been completely off the table for him; he was about to remedy that and hoped to God some of this crazy aggressive anger that had been building up for weeks would subside.

He couldn't do this shit anymore with her, his life had become one mass of up and down emotional bullshit. His head was all over the place to the point he acted like he had PMS like a fucking woman on a daily basis. She drove him nuts, yet he couldn't stay away from her. He loved her, yet he wished he could walk away and never see her again. He didn't know which way was up or down, but he knew one thing—he couldn't bear the thought of firing her and starting over with a new PA, so he had to sort this another way.

Hunter had been right about one thing, the lack of sex was screwing with his head, lack of dates and women in general. This wasn't who he was, wasn't who he wanted to be anymore. He would get his ass off this infernal boat and away from her for a few days. Hunter had already agreed he would look after her should Jake take off, and he was going to screw himself back to sanity with as many women as it took. Hell, he might even go back to the days of more than one at a time if it eased his pain.

Emma had only seen that version of him, so what difference would it make if he went back to it? She had no idea of how much he had changed his lifestyle for her, she didn't see the lack of parties and booze, the lack of women. She only saw what he wanted her to see and lately, it had been a moody fucker who was useless at his job and all over the place. No more. Jake was taking his heart and his goddamn life back.

He picked up his phone from the docking station and skimmed the names until he came to one in particular, hit call and stuck it to his ear. Every part of his gut was trying to stop this insanity, but he had made his mind up and pushed down all the guilt he was feeling to the back of his mind.

"Hello." The female voice that answered sounded surprised to hear from him after so long, but he didn't care, he had chosen her because he knew she would be up for it and available.

"Hey, Brianne, long time no see. Thought I would call and see if you were still up for partying," Jake said smoothly, old Casanova coming out to play effortlessly. He may have been a complete mess around Emma, but with other women, he had no problem at all. He knew how to play them, and he had always done it well. He had zero nervousness about booty calls.

"Of course, for you, Jake, I would literally drop everything." She purred, unable to contain her excitement, and the lust-fueled husk to her tone now. Jake knew he had her right where he wanted. Brianne, from the first time he had met her in a downtown bar, had been hot for him. Obviously so.

"I'm heading home in a few minutes, flight back from a little trip so you could meet me at my apartment tonight, take it from there." He moved his phone from his ear as he hauled off his shirt to get changed, mind already making plans to get the hell out of here.

Carrero Bonus Book 1 ~ Jake's View

"Definitely, baby, I'll be naked and waiting for you, sexy. Do you want me to bring some booze?" She giggled girlishly, doing nothing at all for his libido but he played along.

"Sure, whatever you want, I don't plan on much sleep," he growled sexily and hauled on a new shirt with one hand awkwardly, trying not to picture Emma with every word out of his goddamn mouth. He also couldn't shift the feeling that right now he was a disgusting human being who had never deserved Emma in the first place and this right here proved it. He shoved the sickening lump aside and focused on Brianne.

"Sounds like my kind of party, I can't wait to see you again, it's been far too long, Jakey baby." She once again purred down the line, and he could almost picture her getting wet for him. Girls were too damn easy, maybe that's why he had fallen hard for Emma. She had been the first real challenge to come along in a very long time, the first woman to not drop her panties at the first smile. The first girl that had made him feel something for her that wasn't just lust.

"Cool, so ... laters then. I'll be home around five I guess." He flipped the phone to his other shoulder as he buttoned up his shirt. Not really feeling the same thrill he used too at hooking up with someone as hot and wild as Brianne, but he figured once he got home and had her naked it would all fall into place. Brianne was one of the more adventurous ex-playmates. She was up for any kind of sex and liked to be dominated roughly. Right about now Jake needed to expel a little aggression and doing it sexually was his idea of the perfect solution. He wasn't against a little bit of rough and ready, she liked bondage too and he sure as hell had no problem with being dominant in bed.

"Laters, baby ... a lot of laters." She giggled sexily and

then he hung up, he wasn't much for unnecessary small talk and threw his cell on the bed as he continued to get ready.

* * *

Jake headed up on deck looking for Emma half an hour later, changed into a black fitted shirt and jeans, his usual *ready to party* look. With shades on and a grim expression on his face and a mood to match. He saw her lounging with Leila and called her over, pushing down the ache inside at the sight of her.

"Emma, I need you a second." His tone was emotionless and borderline pissed, guilt trying to push into his mood, but he stuffed it back down knowing he had to stay in this frame of mind to do this. He gestured her to follow him as he turned and headed away from prying eyes, she followed obediently, and he tried to ignore every part of his heart trying to soften at her mere presence.

No more of this wimpy shit, Carrero.

They walked down to the lower floor of the boat, he could feel Emma behind him, tense, quiet and uncertain, but he had to do this for his own sanity. He had to maintain this anger and mood and leave. Leave her and this stupid infatuation behind so he could go back to just working with her.

"I'm leaving for a couple of days; I've left you a credit card in your room in case you want to go out, there's a car on shore that will take you anywhere you want to go." His voice was flat, devoid of emotion and trying so hard to avoid looking at those wounded baby blues that could unravel him in seconds. From the corner of his eye he saw her head snap up and eyes search his face, he got a punch in the gut feeling of regret, but he clenched his fists in defiance and gritted his teeth against it.

"Where are you going? We cleared your schedule for two weeks, so you wouldn't need to go anywhere." She sounded shocked, her voice slightly higher and faster than normal. He could feel the tension and fear coming from her that he was leaving her alone with these people, but he knew Leila would take care of her and Hunter was back tonight and had sworn with his life to watch over her. To make sure no one else tried anything, and that she had a relaxing end to the trip. He felt like an asshole to be leaving her though, he had promised he would take care of her, and he was being a dickhead by not doing that. She had to know this was the best for both of them though.

"Change of plan ... try to relax and have fun, if you can," he said it angrily, at himself, not her. She was looking at him more and more like she was about to cry, and he just felt like punching himself in the face. Anger ripping through him at a hundred miles an hour and worsening his mood.

I'm sorry, bambino.

"Do you need me to come?" she replied coolly in her PA tone. It wasn't what he wanted, but it made this easier on him, closing her out. Taking the feeling out of the conversation and it just reminded him of the fact that this would always be her. She would never love him.

"No, I don't," he replied coldly, fully resigned that what he was doing was right.

"Jake, you pay me to be at your beck and call and go with you at a moment's notice," she retorted haughtily, mannerisms back and the tight lift of that defiant chin. He took a moment to look at that face as a reminder that he would never cross this line again. Every part of him hurting

Jake & Emma

to the point he just felt desolation again.

"I don't pay you to watch me fuck other women, Emma," he snarled at her nastily, frustration making him react. Regretting it as soon as it was out of his mouth but not willing to apologize over this and show any weakness. If he wanted professionalism back, then he had to make her hate him a little bit, even if it killed him.

Emma looked shocked and a little hurt and the urge to take it all back hit him harder, only giving him more resolve to be harsher to kill this friendship the coldest way and be done with it. He looked away from those endless sea eyes that ripped his heart from his chest and hardened his face.

"I'm redefining the boundaries of our relationship— uncrossing the line. That's what you called it, right?" He tossed back casually, avoiding looking at that beautiful face, he couldn't keep this up with her so close.

Don't hate me, miele, just understand this is for the best.

"You think going off to screw someone will uncross that line?" Her words sounded pained, quiet and for a moment Jake doubted all of it. Doubted her feelings and doubted his whole stupid plan. The urge to tell her he didn't mean any of it, to turn and wrap his arms around her and beg forgiveness for being a prick was strong. He would call Brianne in a second and cancel if he thought for one moment Emma would love him back. He turned and saw only cool PA facing him, hands clasped at her waist and a raised brow that contradicted everything.

"It's a start." He turned away in disappointment, heart hitting the floor once again as he led her into his room and pulled a case from the cupboard. He had packed a flight bag already and needed only a few clothes.

"Got over your little break, I see." She sounded cold,

reminding him of admitting to a lack of sex at that charity dance.

"I think that's probably the reason for the latest tension; I need to go let off steam." He smirked icily, glad to have an excuse to cool things between them if he was being honest. He couldn't, in all honesty, keep doing this to himself anymore. His body wasn't built for long periods of celibacy, and his shitty moods and fuzzy head might actually improve. She was watching him with a cool expression, poised and motionless as though observing a naughty child carrying out a punishment, that whole school Miss thing going on. He tried not to look at her, he didn't want to remember her this way anymore. Soft hair and pretty dresses, tanned and beautiful. He would see her back at work, back in tight tailoring and her no-nonsense mask on and take it from there.

"Enjoy yourself." She turned on her heel, a slightly pinched expression that only riled him more, but didn't leave.

"Don't miss me while I'm gone, *tesoro mio*." Jake smiled in full Casanova charm, he all but winked at her. Laying it on thick. "I'm sure you'll find something exciting to do." He was back to focusing on packing, but his voice was flat and emotionless, the cruel and harsh words had been deliberate. He was severing more than unrequited love, he was severing friendship and placing Emma back on the employee list with everyone else at Carrero Corp. He was done.

"When shall I expect you back, Mr. Carrero?" She seemed to get with the program, returning to her business-like manner and tone. His insides bristling with the change in her but accepting what he had chosen finally. This was the future for Jake and Emma. He should never have ventured down this path to feelings and emotions.

Jake & Emma

"When I'm done … hard to say … it's been a while," he sneered without looking up. Twisting the knife to make sure that he had sealed the fate of their relationship. In turn, he was twisting it in his own chest and repulsed at how he was treating her, how he was being with her. If any other guy had dared be this way to her, he would have broken their neck.

He could see Emma smile his way in her fake office face, the one she used to greet business acquaintances and was distracted by his phone vibrating in his pocket. Swiping it out he saw Brianne's name on the screen and hesitated.

Old Jake had openly dated in front of Emma, had openly had women in the same hotel suites, and if he wanted to go back to that, then he had to ignore how sick to his stomach answering this call in front of her was making him feel and get back to being that guy. He hesitated as his conscience tried to get the better of him, quickly making a decision that he hated. He swiped it and pressed the screen.

"Hi," he answered without looking her way, ignoring the nerves ripping through him or the way his hand started trembling with the effort. He lacked his cocky confidence in answering because right now he felt anything but.

"Hi, baby, it's me again. Just checking if you had left yet as I might meet you at the airport instead." Brianne was trying for sexy and soft and only irritated him, Emma's eyes were boring into him and making him feel about a foot tall. He cursed her internally and wished he had ignored the phone.

"I'll be leaving soon." Jake didn't want to have a conversation right now, and he hoped his tone conveyed that to Brianne.

"Oh, do you have company and can't talk? Sorry, I just

missed your voice, it's beyond sexy, and I am so excited about seeing you." She purred irritatingly, and Jake had to steel the urge to tell her to forget all of this.

"Yeah, I missed you too, *bambino*," he said flatly, still feeling Emma's presence burning into him like rays from the sun, he wanted to just curl up and die about now.

"Okay, well my flight gets in around four, so I may hang around at the airfield for you if that's okay?"

"I'll meet you there," Jake said quickly and didn't wait for her reply just hung up quickly to stop the way his throat was trying to strangle him to death with guilt. He slid his phone back into his pocket and couldn't look at her at all, every part of him felt like a complete shithead as though he was openly cheating on her. In his own head, he was, and it had the ability to stop it all if he let it.

Fuck.

"Who?" Emma blurted out and caused another slice to his heart. He couldn't tell her it was the girl he used to replace her so many times when she first started working for him. Brianne was small, blonde and could have been Emma's sister to look at, but she didn't need to know that.

"No one you know. Old flame." He closed his case, throwing her a fiery look, willing her to back off and not pursue this agony.

"If that will be all, Mr. Carrero, I'll leave you to it," Emma said icily and threw him a look that translated to nothing at all, completely deadpan. She was stiff and devoid of emotion. Sad that he had made it happen this way, pushed her to this version of her that she hadn't been since the first week he had known her, but this is who he needed to see from now on.

"Tell the others, after I'm gone, I had to go away for a

couple of days." He was picking up his case, his body stiff with tension and he just had to get out, he couldn't breathe now it was getting closer to leaving her. He was slowly suffocating and on the verge of some sort of anxiety attack.

"What reason shall I give?" She was painfully polite and factual. Another nail in the coffin of his heart.

"I don't give a shit, Emma … the truth for all I care." He flexed his eyebrows sardonically at her, really completely done.

Jake lifted his bags and strolled out purposely past her, not looking her way again and determined to just go and be done with it. The sooner he put distance between them the sooner he would be able to think straight and start rationalizing all of this. He could start to move on and no longer initiate anything non-business related with her.

He felt her follow him down the hall and willed her not to … to stay back and give his heart a chance at letting go of her, he was weakening with every step toward the back of the boat, doubts flooding in and that inner part of him that eternally wanted to protect her clawing him back. To stop, to go back and just get on his knees and beg her to forgive him for being an asshole, but he couldn't.

He knew all it would take was her following him here and one sad look, one sad fucking set of baby blues his way and he would bail on all of this because, like it or not, he fucking loved her, and the last thing he wanted to be doing right now was leaving her for anything in the world. It took all of his strength to walk the last steps and hand his bag to the waiting crewman he had told to get the boat ready. If she came out now he was done for, he knew how weak he was when it came to her, but she didn't.

She had retreated before he hit the open air and had

probably gone back on deck. She had let him go because she had never loved him and as much as he hated himself for doing this it had never been so fucking right. She had made it clear, and he loved her enough to let her fucking go.

He needed to find his own sanity again, and if he could do that between the legs of Brianne it would be a goddamn start.

* * *

By the time the plane touched down in New York Jake was beyond drunk, he had hit the booze hard on the four-hour flight and was at the point of seeing double. He had tried to drown his sorrows and give himself enough Dutch courage to see this through and gone way overboard. He had been consumed with her, memories of kissing her, aching to go back and just stop this bullshit.

God, he missed her already.

Just being away, the miles widening, had been torture for him, and instead of distance giving him the ability to breathe he had felt each mile choking him to near strangulation. He was so fucked over this girl and out of control. Every part of him wanted to turn around and go back. He had pulled up her name on his phone a hundred times and just stared at it, stopping himself from drunk dialing her and telling her he was an asshole because he fucking loved her to death. And he did … all-consuming, every single aching part of him loved her beyond anything he could ever explain. She was his world whether she wanted to be or not and he was a major idiot for letting it get this far.

He hovered over the song he had pulled from his iTunes a hundred times and thought about sending it but didn't.

Apologize—One Republic.

He wanted to tell her he was sorry, he felt like the biggest prick in the world and his heart was wrenched in two at being this way to his angel. His beautiful perfect fucking little angel.

God, he was so fucking drunk.

Getting off the plane had been an ordeal, he hadn't been this smashed in a long time and almost fell down the steps onto the runway in front of Jefferson. He casually came and helped Jake walk to the car with a silent unamused expression on his fatherly face. Jefferson knew better than to say anything; he had been there through Jake's wild years and tended to let him get whatever was eating him out of his system in any way that Jake felt necessary. He just helped Jake get into the car and almost groaned when he saw Brianne already there and grinning his way. She really did look like Emma in a devastating way, but she wasn't her.

No one would ever compare to her even if they were fucking twins who had been separated at birth.

Fuck.

He realized the privacy panel on the limo was already up and groaned, he knew only too well what that meant and didn't have to even look to find she was naked under her fur coat as Jefferson closed the door on them, locking him in his dark hell with a girl who was only focused on sex. Jake was seriously regretting this all over and laid his head back on the seat and just closed his eyes.

"You smell like booze, Jakey baby, did you start without me?" She smiled and crawled over suggestively to straddle his lap as the car moved off. Jake didn't have the energy to react. He just tried to not see Emma in his mind's eye as small hands ran up his abdomen and chest and started

Carrero Bonus Book 1 ~ Jake's View

unbuttoning his shirt. He was no stranger to sex in the back of his cars but right now he didn't care if he never had sex again as long as she let him sleep this off. She tried to kiss him on the mouth, but he turned away. She wasn't her, she didn't kiss like her. He wanted Emma.

"Hmm, yeah." Jake was trying to just sleep, his swimming head trying to give into the darkness, the only thing stopping him was the probing hands on his body or the small wet mouth now moving across his neck and collar bone as she exposed skin. Jake couldn't deny his body was reacting, but he also couldn't deny the whole fucking time he was seeing and hearing Emma in his head. Closing off Brianne completely and just letting his head go any route it wanted. He was definitely getting hard with the writhing, small body on top of him and his hands automatically slid up naked legs under a fur coat to find soft naked skin and curves.

He opened eyes and looked down at the blonde hair across his chest as she licked and nibbled her way down, breathing in her musky perfume and instantly hating that it wasn't tropical or sweet. It was all wrong for how she looked.

Her body ducked lower, and she started unbuttoning his pants, horny Jake starting to take control of his mind and with a visual so Emma-like he couldn't help but react. He shoved her back and helped speed the way, unbuttoning and yanking them down until he was fully exposed and ignoring her face. If he looked at her he would know it wasn't her and wouldn't be able to do this. He closed his eyes again and relaxed into her mouth devouring him.

Pleasure waving up his limbs and the amazing sensation of a hot wet mouth on a part of him that had been severely neglected. She was good at doing this and soon had him reaching that pinnacle of release far too quickly, he came in her mouth, and only for a second felt remorse at doing something so dirty to his beautiful angel. Looking down and seeing Brianne licking her lips back at him. He pushed down the surge of anger and looked away from her again. So goddamn conflicted.

Closing his eyes forcefully as she let her hand bring him back for a second round, her body fully naked now she had let her coat slide down to the floor, the motion of the car only added to how quickly she was getting him turned back on.

Deciding to take matters into his own hands he shoved her off him onto the seat. Facially she didn't have Emma's beauty, and he didn't want to fuck anyone else. So, Jake did the only thing he could, he turned her around and pushed her hard against the seat with every intention of abusing this body until every part of his mind that wanted Emma in every way was satisfied. This is why he had chosen Brianne. From behind she was almost her, and she had no boundaries in the ways she would let him fuck her, she didn't care how rough or how many times as long as it was him. Brianne was one of those all consumed by Jake kind of women and it would serve his purpose tonight. Pushing her into the leather he got up behind her and smacked her hard across the ass. Leaving his mark with satisfaction before leaning in to wipe Emma out of his head for good.

* * *

"Take her home." Jake barked at Jefferson as he got out of the car, Brianne tried to follow, but he pushed her back in by the face cruelly. He had screwed her mercilessly until he came and then he had bluntly told her that she wouldn't be coming home with him. Jake was beyond pissed at himself right about now, and he needed to get the fuck away from her and out of these clothes. He felt dirty and angry and wanted to just go beat the shit out of any mother fucker who looked at him the wrong way.

Sex hadn't done what he wanted—it had given him instant relief for the half hour car journey, he had kept her facing away and let out months of tension and frustration until she screamed. But then he had felt empty and fucked-up and just hated himself more than he did already. Emma wasn't out of his head, instead he had made this a whole lot worse by fucking someone who could so easily be her in his memories and just added to his constant goddamn torture.

He was a complete idiot for choosing Brianne. He should have gone for tall, brunette and skinny as hell.

Brianne tried to grab at his wrist as he maneuvered away and he just glared at her coolly.

"It was a fuck, Brianne, let it go." He yanked his hand free, and all but slammed the door in her face. Jefferson looked at him with a stern expression, but he ignored him. He was still drunk enough to fly off the handle and the last person in the world he wanted to hit was him. Jefferson said nothing but went back to his door and got in. Jake stalked across the car park and toward the elevator in a rage. He was home, back at his apartment yet he didn't want to be here anymore.

He had royally just fucked himself up more in the head. Pressing his penthouse floor code into the keypad, he leaned back against the elevator with a sigh. He wouldn't stay in New York, he would go stay with Arrick in LA for a few days and get his head straight. His brother was only young, but he had a wisdom that sometimes made more sense than Hunter's. He knew women just as well as Jake did and maybe time with his brother and no women at all was what he really needed to do. Sex had cured nothing, just made him realize until he no longer loved Emma, then he would never want to have sex with another woman again. She was it for him, no one would ever compare, and until he stopped looking at her that way then he would forget about sex. Brianne was a mistake, and he had never felt this much regret and guilt in his life. It was eating at him mercilessly and all he wanted to do was pass out and forget all about it, forget the last half an hour and forget the one woman who relentlessly tortured his mind to near insanity.

The Carrero Influence
~ The Elevator Scene ~

Jake walked out of the boardroom meeting without any clue as to what he had just sat and endured for the last hour. Margo had been glaring his way and nudging him with her foot under the table every few minutes and making him all the more aware of how 'out of it' he was. He had been this way ever since his father's email had come in, informing him that Emma was back in his building; Back within reach and he had no idea how to handle it. He didn't know if he should be happy or panicked that he could just see her around his building again, he wasn't sure how the hell to feel about it but couldn't deny the slight feeling of hope in his chest that he could bump into her.

If he was being honest, he hadn't had his head in the game for weeks, not since he had sent her away and today was just another prime example of how 'not well' he was doing without her in his life.

Traipsing behind a couple of his colleagues toward the bank of elevators, he tried like hell to focus on his afternoon

Jake & Emma

schedule. He knew he had a one-to-one with the head of finance over the Hunter-Carrero merger, but for the life of him, he couldn't remember why.

"I'll see you upstairs in a bit." Margo smiled his way from walking beside him, she was rifling through files from the meeting and frowning his way.

"Where you going?" He looked at her blankly, trying like hell to act like a functioning human being instead of the mindless zombie of the past few days. Honestly … few weeks.

"To take these to Brandon." She stared at him deadpan. "Your lawyer." Again, staring like he had two heads. He just stared back completely clueless, and she sighed heavily.

"Well it's just as well one of us was paying attention to the bloody contracts you just signed off on then, isn't it? Jake, for the love of God, go see her, I don't know how much more of this I can endure." She gave him a stern look, sighed, and kissed him on the cheek in her motherly fashion before smoothing down his lapel with her free hand and waving as she walked off. He watched her go feeling even more space cadet and completely out of touch with reality.

So, you signed off on contracts? Idiot!

He heard the elevator ping and open somewhere in front of the men crowding before him and watched them all file into it, sighing and looking back toward Margo for a moment as she disappeared down the hall, he contemplated if she was right. If seeing Emma again would get him out of this funk or if it would just make it all worse.

God, he missed her so fucking much.

Waiting for them all to clear he walked forward to follow them into the elevator and immediately felt his heart thud through his chest. As though some unearthly force had just conjured her up for him out of nowhere because he had

160

Carrero Bonus Book 1 ~ Jake's View

dared to think it. His eyes met hers as soon as he stepped foot inside. Some force of nature making sure he connected with her as soon as he had even walked into the damn thing. She was near the back, behind a bunch of employees and those baby blues met his for a mere second with all the force of a tidal wave. He couldn't breathe.

She was wearing her light-gray tailored jacket and pencil skirt from the first time he had ever laid eyes on her, over a pale-pink silk blouse but with her soft hair still loose, still waves of perfection and a golden halo around that perfect face. It was all a little too painful to bear after weeks of only conjuring her up in his head, and he turned as he found a spot to stand, putting her behind him so he could think about how to handle this. His stomach was churning, a deep painful ache in his chest that made it near impossible to pretend she wasn't so close. Every part of him straining and aching to just turn and look at her, he wanted to hear her voice, see her smile.

She was beautiful, stunning, still his angel.

The elevator stopped, and some men shuffled in and out, he moved further back, still just focusing on his breathing and scrambling thoughts, staring straight ahead for a little control and wondering what he should say to her. He wanted to say something, anything, but he was temporarily rendered mute. Her perfume filling the air around him, he couldn't move, feet locked to the ground and unable to relax at all. She was close enough to just reach out and touch if he turned to look at her, but he just couldn't. It hurt too damn much and being back with her only highlighted how much he was still crazy in love with her. He hadn't moved on in any way at all and this just reminded him of how much his life was completely fucked without her.

More people moved in at the next stop, and he had to

shuffle back, closer to her, her perfume getting clearer and causing him considerable pain. He could feel her, the heat of her body in the elevator despite the other people and he was aware of only her and her proximity. He was almost beside her now, almost shoulder to shoulder save for a gap being forced between them by the man standing just in front of them, he glanced her way warily. His mind just wanting to look at her again and caught those beautiful blues as she did the same thing.

Fuck.

It was like a thunderbolt to his heart and when she looked away quickly and stared at the floor, he couldn't help the overwhelming need and longing to just step forward and touch her. To lift her chin up and just stare at her and tell her he wanted her back in his life. He needed her in his life. Instead, he stared forward at the doors like a coward, trying to rein it all in and losing sight of anyone else in here apart from her and the sheer agony of this.

Say something to her, stop being an asshole and speak.

The lift chimed, and he saw her move to go, his heart pounding erratically and a mild panic set in at the thought of her going, of seeing her leave without anything from him. No words, no smiles.

You're a fucking asshole, Carrero—speak to her!

She had to squeeze past people in front to go, and she brushed against him lightly causing a surge of electricity and a major pang of longing. It was a brief touch, but it rendered him completely useless. Looking at her hopelessly and just aching to reach out and pull her against him. His tongue working loose in a last-ditch effort as she caught his eye momentarily. She was the only girl he had ever met who could turn him to mush with just a look at those perfect almond eyes that turned his knees weak.

"Miss Anderson," he said quietly and politely, trying for a smile that was genuine and just feeling like he was stiff and disconnected. Her beauty floored him, her eyes meeting his had made him unable to function, and her perfume would stay in his head for eternity at this rate.

I love you, bambino, and I fucking miss you so much that I can't bear this.

"Mr. Carrero." She breathed back, no smile, no emotion just a cold tone and obviously still hurt over his betrayal. He couldn't blame her, she had been his right hand, and he had severed it and sent her off to work in a place he knew she probably would have hated. They had crossed a line by having sex, but it had been the best moment of his life, one night that would haunt him forever and he never wanted to lose the memory of what she felt like. He wanted to replay it for an eternity and would never regret being with her.

To her though, he had done what he always did, he had fucked her and disposed of her. As much as it pained him to have her think that way he knew it was for the best, for both of them.

He had hurt her, cut her off, and disconnected from her in the worst possible way for his own sanity, and looking at the cool way she hurriedly walked out of the elevator without a backward glance he, knew he deserved her icing him out. He had been a shithead and a coward and sent her away rather than keep going through the torture of being around her. He just wished that seeing her again wasn't like a stake being driven through his heart over and over and he slumped against the back wall as the doors closed on the most beautiful view he had ever seen.

Back to reality, Carrero. You never fucking had her. You never deserved her.

The Carrero Influence

~ **The Dance** ~

Jake shifted in his seat for the millionth time and tried once more to get his brain to focus on the laptop on the highly polished walnut surface. He just couldn't keep himself on track lately.

The sound of a female clearing her throat startled him to look up and the impatient stance of Margo waving a piece of paper with a raised eyebrow suggested she had been talking to him while he was zoned out.

"Sorry. What?" He frowned and sighed heavily, pushing himself back into his molded leather chair and rolled up his shirt sleeves in agitation.

"For God's sake, Jacob. I've been here for three minutes talking at you. You need to just bloody well call her." Margo's stern tone did nothing to help his current mood, and he just shifted forward again to try to ignore that intent, chastising glare. He went to his laptop, ducking his head in an attempt to dodge her blue eyes and typed something aimlessly.

Jake & Emma

"Don't know what you're talking about. And less of the Jacob." He shrugged with one shoulder and pushed images of Emma from his head for the millionth time. He wondered if maybe he should remind Margo that personal relationship aside, he was still her boss.

Damn Emma for always being inside his head.

"Sure! Because moping around like a love-sick kid for weeks on end after impulsively firing the best assistant you ever had means nothing. Look … you may not want to spell things out to me, but it is pretty obvious you crossed the line with her, problem being that for some stupid reason you then let her go, or should I say pushed her away." Margo moved toward him and perched her tight-skirted ass on his desk the way Emma used to do anytime they had time in here.

He shook his head to dislodge it from his mind's eye and instead went back to typing pointless words on a ruined document.

"Stop that." Margo covered his hand with hers and stopped him from continuing. He yanked his hands free, agitated, pushing back his chair and getting up to walk up and down the length of his windows, finding no peace in the skyline out there for once.

"I didn't just let her go, it was never going to be anything more for her, so I stopped myself from crossing that line again. Why are we even talking about this? Is there something I can actually help you with?" He stomped back to his seat, not sure what the hell he was even doing and slumped back down, creasing his shirt and not giving a damn. Running his fingers through his cropped hair and frowning once more at the stupid document on screen.

"You can figure out what you're doing with these then.

Deal with it yourself. I do not happen to like dealing with the Giovanni stubbornness in you, short-sighted and pig-headed to boot!" She threw the paper she had been waving around in her hand on top of his laptop keyboard distastefully. Taking them idly he noticed tickets stapled to the top corner with Emma's name printed on. He looked up at her quizzically with a frown.

"What are they?" He genuinely had no clue.

"Tickets to that bloody dance you wanted all the staff to attend. I suggest she gets them and decides for herself if she wants to see you." Margo didn't wait for a response, she was turning on her heel and moodily trotting out on stilettos that made an echoing clip-clop at speed. She was still pissed at him, had been since she came back and found out what he had done concerning Emma.

"Margo? What the hell?" It was futile, she was waving him away and playing deaf. She kicked his outer door shut to emphasize that she was still seriously furious with him. He had endured weeks of her snippy attitude and stern chastising already, he had no clue why he hadn't fired her ass for it. Probably because deep down he knew he deserved it, he had behaved like an asshole and Margo was only thinking about Emma and how this must hurt her. All he had thought about since her departure was how much this must be hurting her.

He lifted the tickets again and read over the name printed clearly in gold foiling, a thumb tracing her first name slowly as that familiar ache in his heart panged to the forefront. Without hesitation, he hit his intercom buzzer to Margo's desk.

"Send them to her as soon as you can." He let it go without expecting a response, chucked them back to the outer part of his desk and sank back covering his face with the back of his hands and sighing. He had no idea if she would even go to the dance but part of him wanted it to be her choice if she did. He wanted to see her, yet he didn't, because it would hurt either way.

The door to his office opened almost instantly, the clip-clop of heels, the swish of fabric and waft of Margo's perfume, by the time he moved his hands she was retreating to her own part of the office carrying the sheet of paper and still freezing him out. He rolled his eyes and thought better of trying to chastise her about this ongoing behavior. Margo was like a second mother to him and his own mother would probably be acting the same way right about now. He had better get used to her angry standoff because he knew she wasn't going to let up on him anytime soon.

* * *

Jake pulled at the collar off his tux repeatedly, trying to stop the choking sensation of wearing a bow tie and ignored the glances his way. He had been here only minutes and already showing up single was attracting way too much attention, probably because he had never come to an event dateless.

He could feel the judgmental and surprised looks from the array of rich and minor celebrities in the ballroom, less than an hour after opening and he already hated it here.

"Hola!" Leila butted into his thoughts and slid an arm through his confidently. "Looking as suave as always my lovely." She grinned up at him with that cheeky youthful face he adored like a sister and just yanked at his collar once more, stifling in this crowded ballroom and hating having to dress up in this monkey suit. She pulled his hand away and started to fix his crooked bow tie for him, slapping his hand down when he tried again to get at his top button.

"You look nice, classy dress." His eyes swept the long black glittering ball gown with the peak of pink at the neckline while she fussed over him, typically Leila.

"You brush up pretty well for a skinny tomboy."

He was relieved to be released when she had done fluffing him over.

"Shut up, loser." Leila nipped his bicep with her overly long manicured nails, arm slid back into place inside his and threw him a suddenly serious look. "She's coming you know? She texted me, I don't think she knows that I know."

Jake swallowed hard, an impulsive response he had no control over, frowning as the stomach-lurching sensations hit him again. This had been happening all day.

"What do you expect me to say to that?" He focused his gaze across the room, uncomfortable with this topic of conversation and already wishing he had never confided in Leila about any of this over the phone the night before. She was unpredictable sometimes, and he knew she rooted for Emma like no other. She had been one of the worst to give him a hard time about sending her away.

"I expect you to look happy at least, Jake, you need to tell her how you feel." Jake held his hand up and hushed her, it was all new to Leila and nothing he had not heard before from Margo, his mother and hell, even Daniel.

"Look. Stop. Not the time or place, Leila, so get any dumb thoughts out of your head about interfering in this." He threw her a warning eyebrow raise and hated that her stubborn jut of the chin became more prominent. He had no energy for a Leila maneuver tonight.

"Oh, for God's sake! Look just stop being arsey as fuck and try to act like you're happy to see her when she gets here. She did nothing wrong, Jake, and you need to man up and stop sulking when someone mentions her name." Leila jutted her hip out and almost slammed her hand on it.

Jake glared at her, his own mood taking a nose dive, a skill Leila had since childhood.

"You can stop looking at me like that too or else I'll poke you in the eye with my new nails. Do you like them by the way? Extra sharp in case your asshole best mate shows up to piss me off." She swayed around her sparkling pink nails.

"Stunning," Jake replied flatly and then dodged her pretend cat-like claw aimed at his face. Leila was one of those annoying friends that you let get away with murder because they were genuinely more family than friend. At times though he just wanted to strangle her, tonight was one of those nights after a full day of her constant texts, questions and lectures.

"I can see you watching for her you know." Leila cut in, looking at him smugly and lifting one eyebrow as she edged in close. Not that it made a difference as she hadn't bothered to lower her voice over the in-house orchestra blaring some Mozart.

"Jesus! Leila, for fuck's sake." He lowered his voice when he realized he had just snapped loudly, and people were looking his way. "I'm going to the bar, you can stay here and piss someone else off for a change." He dropped her arm from his and moved away, striding aggressively in the direction of hordes of overly dressed up strangers in a bid to get some head space. He hated that she was right though, he had been scanning the crowd ever since he got here. On edge, nervous and tense and just watching for the one girl in the world that he couldn't mentally escape from. He had been a fool to kiss her only days ago, to keep ending up with her no matter how hard he tried to stay away. He knew he was only torturing himself and dragging this out.

The inner floor was full of people milling around in various degrees of expensive formal wear. The music loud and invading from the full orchestra as he pushed through people that wanted to cling to him and bask in his presence.

Jake strode purposefully through a heavy crowd of glittering women in floor-length dresses, coming out into a clearing with a side step away from an overeager pair of hands and walked smack bang into the one face that made his heart stop beating.

Emma walked into the clearing at the exact moment he did, and they both just seemed to stop and stare at each another, his heart pounding erratically as it recovered, his breathing becoming shallow. She looked beautiful, beyond his wildest dreams. Wearing a fitted floor-length red dress that left little to his imagination and seemed to defy gravity while clinging to her bust and waist. He could barely swallow, taking in every perfect flawless curve up to the face of perfection and that wild hair he just wanted to tangle around his fingers at every opportunity. She looked like a Hollywood star from the fifties, perfection in every way and effortless grace. She stood out from everyone in this room, hell, to him she stood out from every single woman in the world. She always had.

Fuck.

They stood motionless, feet apart. Tension crackling in the air between them and neither seemed to know how to react or what to say. All Jake could think about was what it was like to have her in his arms, to feel her against him and how much he wanted to touch her right now.

"Oh, my God, Emma!" Leila's excitable voice grabbed her attention as she dove on Emma from the right of Jake;

she had obviously followed him when he headed to the bar. Throwing herself around Emma, who was only inches taller and almost hauling her off her shoes. Jake didn't move, just continued to watch her, unable to tear his eyes from that face that could stop the world from turning. He didn't care that the women just to his left were trying to capture his attention subtly.

"Whoa, Leila," Emma choked, laughter breaking over her delicate face and changing the apprehension to knock out beauty. Jake stiffened, trying to keep his emotions in check and trying to hide any reactions she caused him. Just being this close to her, unable to just be how they used to be was complete agony and his heart had continued some sort of rumba inside his chest.

"I've missed you, millions! Emails are not the same, Miss Ems. You look freaking sensational!" Leila spun Emma round and sent her reeling, losing her footing on high shoes, Jake moved swiftly forward and caught her mid tumble. Pulling her against him despite every one of his senses telling him to let her go. The feel of her body against his sent an electric jolt through him, heating his blood and making his stomach lurch with emotion. She smelled better than good and her scent would only keep haunting him even after he left here, now that he had the smell of her on his tuxedo.

Jake stood her up carefully, holding her upper arms until she found her footing once more and released her as soon as she was steady. He knew the danger of keeping her close, and he just couldn't handle her proximity with her looking as devastating as she did tonight.

"Careful, Leila." Jake scorned Leila, catching the wicked gleam in her eye of a calculated plot she had brewed up. Jake narrowed his eyes at her and shook his head over the top of Emma. Moving to look away as she turned back to him, in case she saw what was transpiring. She seemed to focus on him for a moment and as much as he wanted to just turn back and dive into those baby blue eyes, he couldn't bear it.

"I can't help being so happy to see her, Jake, you keep her hidden from me." She grinned wickedly at him, messages in their silent communication they had perfected from years of being friends. Jake tried hard not to glare and instead threw her a slight frown and a subtle warning to back off.

"I've been working." Emma looked quickly from Leila to him and back, an air of confusion about her, but she recovered quickly and smiled softly. Jake had to tear his eyes from that perfect red-lipped smile and push out thoughts of kissing her over and over again. She wasn't normally one for bold lipstick, normally subtle shades and he was finding it near impossible to stop looking at the perfect pout and curve of lips so obviously made for passion. Music overtook the conversation as the band heated up a notch, a slow ballad coming across the air, making conversation near impossible.

"Oh, I promised someone a first slow dance." Leila turned Emma harshly, shoving her into Jake hard with that wicked smile aimed right at him, a twinkle of trouble in her eye.

His arms automatically caught her and pulled her into his chest, throwing Leila a look of complete intolerance; he would be having words with her later. Jake quickly put Emma upright and back on her own feet as her perfume hit him again, too much for him to handle, combined with how good touching her always felt. He shifted her away, so he could gain some distance and regain control of his equilibrium.

"Keep her warm for me until I come back, Jacob!" Leila grinned cheekily and took off at speed, knowing that Jake was probably about to explode and hightailing it so she could leave them alone. She knew there would be repercussions later, but she didn't really care.

"That girl," Jake said tightly, irritation concealed but his anger simmering inside. He avoided looking at Emma, wondering how the hell he could walk away from her and leave her here alone while looking so utterly fucking lost right now. She had an air of Bambi with big eyes and seemed to be suddenly uncomfortable with Leila's departure. Jake couldn't control the stomach punching sensation it gave him.

"You've got to love her though." Emma shrugged nervously, biting on her bottom lip and causing yet another wave of excruciating pain. All her little anxiety tells had always been a point of agony for him, he hated seeing her doing it but right now any little Emma-ism was just killing him more. He missed everything about her so much.

Do you really have no idea how goddamn adorable you are?

The music was moving into full swing as couples moved around them, joining together to sway. Emma went into ultimate fidget mode almost immediately, twirling her hair like she always did when she was tense, looking around for an escape route and pretty much making him feel like the biggest asshole known to man. He watched her hand in her hair intensely for a second, lost in so many thoughts and memories, hating the habit yet pining for the familiarness of it. He realized she had caught his look, misunderstood what it meant and yanked her fingers out of her hair like a scolded child.

Great! Another notch of assholeness.

Jake frowned and looked about the floor, making a decision almost instantly.

"Want to dance with me, Anderson?" He had no clue

Carrero Bonus Book 1 ~ Jake's View

why he thought this was the best course of action, all he knew was that he didn't want to walk away and leave her here and had no desire to see anyone else dance with her. He would kick seven shades of shit out of any guy who dared touch her. She looked momentarily shocked, color draining from her face a little and her fingers twitched as though aching to be back in her hair. Jake felt a warmth of compassion, an old memory of her looking this unsure and untrusting of his intentions once before.

"I don't bite." Jake smiled at the memory of a long-ago moment in his office. Emma seemed to register the memory too, a small smile warming her mouth and looked a little less shell shocked.

Jake didn't wait for an answer; his body had been aching to be with hers for so long that it was almost impulsive to just reach for her. Pulling her close by the wrist, encircling her dainty smooth skin and bracing himself for the onslaught of emotions that hit him with her nearness.

Emma automatically slipped into dance pose, hand in his and the other on his chest to stop the collision from the suddenness of his maneuver. Her palm was placed directly over his heart and with a searing touch, he was sure she could probably feel how hard and fast his heart was beating. He couldn't tear his eyes from that perfect red mouth as he drew closer. Emma looked stricken suddenly, a mixture of emotions flitting across her face so fast he had no clue what to even think.

"I can't do this," she whispered suddenly, her voice breaking, and he could have sworn he saw a glint of a tear in her eye, but she was turning from him and trying to break free. Jake impulsively caught her chin with his fingers, tilting her back to him so he could try to read what she was feeling. Confused at seeing a look that, to him spelled out complete heartbreak and rendered him almost immobile as he tried to piece together what it meant. Before he had a chance to speak or control the sudden hammering of his chest, she had pulled her hand away and was pushing away from him.

"I need to go." She yanked her chin away, face down so her hair spilled forward to hide her features from him. Jake felt panic rising within him, confusion and emotion consuming him, he stood motionless, unsure how to react as he watched her move away out of sight into the crowds.

Jake's head became a mass of thoughts and feelings all warring for space, chaos clouding logical thought as his body seemed to jolt into a mess of heart-pounding sickening panic. He kept questioning that look, trying to dissect in seconds why she would look at him the way he had been looking at himself in the mirror for weeks. His head skimming through memories and conversations of the last weeks with her, tidbits of clues and puzzle pieces.

He remembered the last song she sent him and reached into his jacket for his phone, looking up to see if she was still close enough to catch and realizing she was completely gone.

Fuck, fuck, fuck.

Jake was glued to the spot, uncertainty keeping him here despite every part of his being screaming at him to go after her. It was then that it hit him, like a sudden lightning bolt moment. He had to know if he was just imagining it or if she could feel the same for him that he did for her. If that's what he just saw in her eyes.

Looking at the phone in his hand he knew the way to ask. Hands shaking, he skimmed songs quickly until he found one which had been plaguing the radio for the last week.

Sending it out into the network and to her phone without hesitation and hoping to God she had her cell with her. He

Carrero Bonus Book 1 ~ Jake's View

had nothing else to lose, he had lost everything when she had walked out of his office and standing there watching her leave was only a harsh reminder that he would never love anyone the way he loved her. He needed to be sure.

Jake Carrero has sent an iTunes gift to Emma Anderson.

The email notice popped up on his phone and his stomach churned with nerves.

Jake Carrero, you sent Jessie Wares—'Say You Love Me'.

He knew there was no backing out of it now, she could only take that song one way and he would finally know for sure if he had ever stood a chance with her. The world seemed to stop around him, music dulling out to nothing, as the rush of blood ran through his ears. Close to his first ever real panic attack, he was sure his heart might explode.

Come on, Emma, any sort of answer, please.

He was staring at his phone, motionless in a sea of dancing bodies and completely unaware of anything except the blank screen in front of him.

It seemed like an eternity before an email notification pinged up on his screen, his heart lurching and his stomach dropping with fear, with trembling hands he hit the screen and opened the email.

Emma Anderson has gifted you an iTunes song.

Emma Anderson has sent you—Paloma Faith—'Only Love Can Hurt Like This'.

Jake's world stopped, a moment of pause as he took this in and it slowly dawned on him what her response meant. He read it twice to be sure before impulse took over and he was moving fast in the direction she left. Body alive with energy and tingling. He was on hyper-drive and determined that his only goal now was finding the girl who was about to be kissed to within an inch of her life. He was soaring, still desperate to push through the crowds and just find her.

Emma loved him. His Emma really loved him, the way he loved her.

His eyes were scanning the floor, people getting in his way were moved with a little force, ignoring people trying to stop him and talk. He just had one thing on his mind and he was damned if anyone was going to get in his way. He needed to find her and just see her, talk to her. Every blonde head and red dress was being assessed as he moved at a fast pace, shrugging off hands and hellos, sliding through groups of people with determination. Not giving a shit at how ignorant he was being.

And then, there she was. Stopping him dead in his tracks, her eyes focused on him at the edge of the dance floor as though she had been waiting for him to find her. Looking like everything in the world that mattered to him, standing stock still only feet away. His entire being halted.

Jake didn't hesitate a moment longer, the look on her face said everything he needed to act. She was wide-eyed and distraught, heartbroken and almost begging him to come to her. Who was he to refuse when all he had ever wanted was for her to want him this way?

His feet had him marching her way, fast long strides to get to his end goal as soon as humanly possible. He didn't stop when he got to her, just intent on his purpose, aching to do what he had planned when he found her.

His hands automatically cupping her face and pulling her to him, cupping her jaw, and meeting her mouth with unleashed force and passion that completely sent his head spiraling and heart soaring. Finally, complete. He kissed her as though his life depended on it, reveling in the way she sagged into him and kissed him back with matched fever. Jake was flying, his heart erratic, and he knew this was all he would ever need, just her and him and the ability to be this way with her. She was his soul.

She clung to him as much as he held her, matching his passion and movement and neither breaking away from the intensity of the meeting for long minutes.

They were breathing hard, oblivious to the room around them and only focused on each other. He couldn't stop himself from kissing her, but he knew he had to do more, he had to tell her how he felt. He had to let her talk and confirm that this was something more than sex or lust. He needed her to know that he was serious about her, that for him, she was his forever. He needed to say the words he had been holding back for months. Jake needed to tell her that he was hopelessly in love with her.

Breaking away finally, only enough to rest his forehead against hers and breathe her in, he just stared into the depths of those cool blue eyes that seemed to see right down into his very soul. Neither seemed to have words, just matched shallow breathing, oblivious to the room and people around them. He didn't care if reporters were taking pictures, or if people were staring right now, all he cared about was her and what she was thinking.

"Come with me?" Jake finally managed a whisper, tearing himself physically away from being so close to her and aching to get her alone. Despite the noise of the orchestra and the hustle and bustle around them, she seemed to hear him loud and clear, never tearing her eyes from his and nodding. Jake couldn't help the surge of happiness running through him, couldn't resist brushing his mouth against hers once more. Emma always tasted sweet, like cakes and candy and her; a heady combination that was addictive to him, he didn't even care if her lipstick was all over him right now.

He let go of her and slid her small dainty hand in his, interlocking fingers possessively and leading the way toward the main entrance fast. He couldn't stop the dizzying euphoria coursing through him or the sense of urgency in getting her alone. He just felt like this was all surreal after what felt like a lifetime of not being able to have her. He was walking on the clouds.

Winding through the crowded room, Jake's impatience was rising with every person who got in his way. Familiar faces stopped them and even though he tried to deflect the attention, he had to stop when flanked by a client who was a little more forceful in getting his attention. The stocky man seemed oblivious to the young, beautiful girl he was so obviously trying to usher out of the room with him. Jake could feel himself almost growling with frustration as he launched into a speech about some funding nonsense for a new venture. Jake glanced down at Emma to check she was okay, to check she was real and this wasn't some weird hallucination. That face looking trustingly up at him only tore at him more and made him more determined to get her alone.

God, I love you so fucking much, bambino.

Jake's attention was pulled back by the gray-haired suit extending a hand, some feeble attempt at agreeing to a lunch date for a business chat. Jake hadn't even been listening, so overly aware of the warm, soft hand in his and the way Emma was curling gently around his side. He wanted to have more contact with her than this. He wanted to wrap himself up in her. Pulling her in closer, Jake tucked her slender arm under his and grasped her hand a little firmer, closer but still not close enough to be able to deal with these idiots holding them up. Right now, he would agree to pitch a million at any stupid idea as long as they shut the fuck up and got out of his way.

Finally, suit moved and Jake made a move to get them going once more, they didn't get far before another one slid in front, blocking their passage. Jake almost yelled at him in sheer frustration.

For fuck's sake.

Impatience and complete frustration had him nodding eagerly, trying to slide past and pulling Emma into him a little forcefully. He was trying to palm the suit off with a hand wave, but he was having none of it.

"So, Mr. Carrero, we could meet up ..." Jake zoned out, focusing only on her, sliding her hand free and instead put an arm around her waist and bodily molded them side by side, she rested her head against his chest impulsively, and he almost melted into a mushy puddle on the floor. She had no idea what she could do to him with minimal effort. Jake kissed her temple, he just wanted to be done here and to be able to get this all out. To look her in the eye and ask her straight out if she wanted to be with him from now until eternity. That's all he could think about.

"Yeah sure, just call my office to make a lunch appointment. Anytime." Jake almost waved the guy out of his face, missing his handshake a little prematurely and just moving to get past quickly, oblivious to the awkwardness he had just caused in the man left flailing hands in mid-air.

Jake pulled Emma with him fast, seeing an opening within the standing people and aiming for it before anyone else snagged him to a standstill. Emma stumbled on her shoes, and he almost cursed at the fact he knew he was practically dragging her, guilt hitting him hard and knocking him for six.

"I'm sorry ... I just need to get you out of here quickly ...

I need us to be alone—to talk." He sounded nervous as hell and maybe he was, all he knew was this place was starting to piss him off and looking for escape was proving to be more difficult than he planned. Getting them finally to the main hall, he looked around for privacy, spying a little door marked staff that was sat ajar and showed a dark unused hall.

Perfect.

Leading the way once more, he slowed down as Emma lifted her dress and seriously thought about scooping her up to carry her for a moment. Looking around at the volume of milling guests he thought better of it and slowed his pace to let her keep up. Looking at her in that dress, her sexy-as-hell shoes peeking out in all their tall stiletto beauty, his body went into immediate hunger overdrive. God, he wanted more than just to kiss her, he wanted her naked and under him. Her shoe choices had always made him horny, she had perfect legs, and he loved nothing more than seeing them slid into shoes like this. If he got her home in this dress, or even out of that dress, those shoes would be staying on.

Checking around he opened the door further into a dim abandoned hall and pulled her inside with him, turning her so he could push her back against the wall behind the cover of the door and unleashing every urge he had been fighting out there to kiss her again. This time the force of all the pent-up lust hit out harder, flooring her with a kiss that sent him into lust overdrive. He could barely control the way she made him feel, the way he wanted her and as she crumbled into him he had to crush her further into the wall to hold her up. His hands slid around her curves, fingers smoothing over sweet warmth.

Sense seemed to catch up with him with the unleashing of pent-up passion and doubts started to creep in. He hadn't let her talk even once since he kissed her, he hadn't let her confirm that she even wanted this.

Isn't this always what I do to her? Push myself onto her with force, so that she can't do anything but play along.

Jake tilted his head back, unable to let her go even though insecurity and doubt were now flooding through his over-wired brain, he was a jumbled mess of emotions and had no way to deal with the flood of self-doubt that had just hit him square in the stomach. He frowned, swallowing down his fear and realizing she still hadn't said anything, just staring at him helplessly and ripping his heart to shreds with silence. It was starting to feel all too familiar and every single instance just like this came flooding to mind. A million rejections that had started with promise.

"I'm waiting on it, Emma." His voice was low and pained, hating himself for his tone and acting this way after the way he had just kissed her. He was an emotional mess and had been for months. He just couldn't bear any of this anymore, and he needed her to just say it.

"On what?" She sounded young and vulnerable, doe-eyed, and meek. He wanted to punch himself in the face for his sudden change toward her, but he couldn't help it. Part of him was back peddling and getting ready for another scene that left him here and Emma walking away, preparing for another stab in the heart.

"The door to hit me in the face again; another reason you think we shouldn't be together." He said it sardonically, his tone flat as though already resigned that this was too good to be true. He felt the overwhelming fear rising up his spine, knowing from experience that her kissing him back meant nothing.

Emma shook her head, her face softening and lifted her fingers to trace the shape of his lips. The touch sending a

Jake & Emma

tingling sensation right through his very soul, catching her hand to press it to his face and commit this moment to memory in case it was the last. Emma smiled at him.

"I'm not going to do that, Jake. I won't push you away again."

Jake felt the inner pain and dread loosen a little, watched the way Emma remained calm and continued to gaze up at him with unveiled adoration. This really was different for her this time. His tense muscles relaxed as a warm realization hit him, he really had her after all. She wasn't running or closing down, she wasn't even pushing him away. Still in his arms and touching him freely.

"I love you … I think I've been in love with you for a very long time." Jake let it out, like a wave of relief, something that had been on his lips for what felt like an eternity and had never had the courage to say to her. Smiling at the release and suddenly not feeling so scared anymore. Emma, however, burst into an instant mess of unexpected tears that shocked him.

Jake pulled her against his chest, confused and a little unsure how he was meant to take that at all. All he could do was hold her, stroke her hair and pray to God she was "happy" crying. Hoping that's what women did anyway.

"I … I …" she stammered and then got even more emotional, falling to pieces in his arms and gripping onto him tightly as flood gates of tears and sobbing opened up. All he could do was cling right back on and bury his face in her hair helplessly. His heart upping a beat and fear coming back to gnaw at his insides. Emma wasn't much of a crier and whenever she did he hated it, made him feel pretty much like it did now, as though his insides were being twisted out in the most excruciating way.

"Don't cry, *bambino* … Please, Emma … I didn't think telling you I loved you would cause this," he said hoarsely, tensing his arms around her and just trying so hard to mold every line and curve to him while supporting her. "Say something."

Anything, please … Tell me you want this.

"I … love … you." It came from her so breathily between sniffs, Jake immediately exhaling complete relief and suddenly aware he had been holding his breath. His body went into instant warm and fuzzy overdrive and for once in his life understood all that girly mushy crap about butterflies and inner tingles. The overwhelming euphoria of three little words from the only person who truly mattered changed everything in that one moment.

Jake lifted her chin gently, unable to stop the goofy happy smile breaking across his face and kissed her softly. He could do this for an eternity and never tire of how good she felt. How kissing her seemed to make the world stop turning and everything make sense. He could kiss Emma every second of every day for a lifetime and know it would always feel this good.

His gentle meeting of the lips set her off again into another flood of hormonal tears, only this time Jake didn't crumble into insecurity, he smiled instead and watched her with a small shake of the head.

"Jesus, Emma … If I'd known this was how it would be, I would've brought some tissues and a lot of chocolate." Tangling his fingers in her soft, silky hair, no longer pained at her tears because he knew sometimes girls cried when they were happy. In this case, he had no doubt his beautiful girl was happy. Her giggle through tears confirmed it and he sighed against her once more.

Jake & Emma

What am I going to do with you?

Emma looked up under lowered lashes, her makeup doing a pretty good job of staying put for the most part, despite the waterworks and smiled at him coyly. It had the same effect as a thud to the chest.

"They're happy tears." She smiled once more, another sniff and some signs of regaining composure. Emma pulled her bag forward and began to search for something, he assumed a tissue, seeing as now her cheeks were starting to get little rivers of diluted black running subtly down them. It only made her even more goddamn adorable to him, and he lifted his hand to her face to start removing the traces of makeup as they fell.

"Should I be crying too then?" He smiled down at her, wiping her cheek with his thumb and then switching tactics to his jacket sleeve and dabbing at her instead. He didn't care if this was a ten-thousand-dollar suit, his baby needed a tissue, and he would let her use his entire shirt if she wanted it. He wiped most of her upset away before caging her in against the wall to just take her in. Every little detail of her in full glory had his heart soaring, he moved in close, so he could breathe her in. Three words had just changed everything between them and now his life was looking a hell of a lot better.

"I don't think I want to see you cry." Emma blinked up at him cutely, a face so innocent and beautiful that he had no resistance to her.

"Good. I'm not much of a crier and you're doing a grand enough job for the both of us. I'm happy though, you have no idea. I never thought we'd get here. I didn't think this was how you felt about me." Jake moved in, wanting contact with her at all times and rested his brow against hers. She leaned up suddenly and bravely and kissed him this time, knocking

Carrero Bonus Book 1 ~ Jake's View

the wind out of him momentarily and pretty much making him the happiest guy on the planet in that second. It only ignited his deep longing for her and passion brimmed in milliseconds, bracing her face to him by sliding his hand behind her neck so he could deepen the kiss and caress her tongue with his. Emma groaned under her breath which in turn made him groan too, still hopeless to how much power she always had over him.

Jake pulled away before he lost all control and ripped her dress open, unable to just break free, he sucked in her bottom lip and gently slid away. He loved the taste of her in every way and could only imagine how much he was going to devour every single inch of her skin when he got her alone.

The way Emma was looking up at him told him that would be sooner rather than later, the unleashed raw look on her face of sheer lust had his body stirring and heat rising within. He wanted her so badly it was almost painful.

"If we keep doing this, then I can promise you I won't be a gentleman for much longer." He warned her, voice soft as his focus stayed on the slightly kiss-swollen set of perfect lips. The red lipstick was still in place and weirdly unsmeared.

"Oh, I always knew you weren't a gentleman." She jested, biting her lip seductively and staring right back at Jake's own mouth. She wasn't helping calm his libido one little bit.

God, I want to kiss you and fuck you nonstop.

"Hey! I've been very well behaved. You have no idea the kind of thoughts that went through my head concerning you." He caught her wrists and pinned them up over her head, loving how it made her both vulnerable and open to his control but the way it made her bust rise up from her

187

dress a little, peeking a little riskily on the verge of overflow. He wanted her naked more than anything and still glued to her body it was really hard to keep the obvious sign under control in his pants.

"None of that surprises me, you and your ex-rated mind. I always knew you had Casanova tendencies." Emma grinned up at him, shifting her pelvis closer and almost nudging him.

"Cheeky!" He threw her a fast, chaste, kiss and let her go, more than aware that he was about to lose his shit and fuck her against the wall if they kept this up. He had little control around her normally, so this was only testing all his powers to the very verge of his limits. "You're beautiful, and you're all mine!"

He moved his body from hers and leaned in for another soft kiss, something he knew would be an addiction from here on in. Having this ability to just kiss her whenever he wanted was like all his birthdays coming at once and he intended to use it to its full potential.

"I'm still mad at you." Emma slid her palms across his stomach, sending shivers of anticipation through him, her hands smoothing within his jacket which was open and sliding up across the muscles in his chest. He had to steel himself against the urge to turn to Jell-O. His eyes followed her progress and the tiny hint of a smile tugged at her lips, he couldn't stop looking at her.

"I don't blame you, *bella.*" He frowned. "I'm mad at me too," Jake replied regretfully, smoothing her hair back behind her ear and taking a moment to focus on untangling a strand from the dangling diamond cluster earring. He needed to calm down his playboy impulses if he was going to romance her into a happy ever after. She wasn't going to be some one-night piece of fun for him; Emma was all he had been waiting for in life. The other half to his soul. He watched her carefully, regret at so many lost months eating at him, knowing if he had just been honest with her long ago then he would have always had her.

Complete idiot.

"Makes a change from being mad at me, I guess." Emma's smile widened to a smirk as he regarded her. Lost in how many times he could have changed the course of their relationship by saying three little words to her.

"I only got mad with you because of how I feel about you, Emma. It was ripping me apart. I didn't know how to behave around you or how to deal with all this crap inside of me. Over-emotional men are just snarky shits." He softly smiled, knowing it was lame as apologies went, but he intended to spend every day for the next hundred years making this up to her.

"I get mad at you because you're an asshole sometimes; nothing to do with emotions or love." She joked, smiling widely with a hint of amusement in those gorgeous pale eyes. She moved to run her fingertips softly across his mouth again, drawing his attention to how perfect they gelled. Each touch tailored to the other almost perfectly and how she could weaken him so easily.

"We need to make this work." Jake sighed. "I can't walk away again … I don't want to. This past month has been unbearable like I had my insides wrenched out."

"Are you asking me to be your PA again?" she asked softly, looking him dead in the eye with a hint of the old Emma confidence seeping back in. He couldn't help but smile at her.

"I'm asking for way more than that, *miele.*" His hands had moved back into that blonde curled hair he loved so much, fingertips grazing her scalp as he entangled its silky smoothness between his fingers. He loved that every time he touched her hair it not only felt good but released more of her delicious scent.

"Tell me what you want from me, be specific." Emma had gone into full-on PA mode, that stern yet inquisitive look, she was waiting for him to lay his cards on the table before she let too much of her own hopes out. Typical Emma, still guarding her heart until she was sure he wasn't going to trample on her.

I love you, bambino.

Jake did not hesitate in doing what she needed.

"I want you … all of you … I want us. Just you and me and no one else. No games, no hiding, no more misunderstandings. I want you to be the one woman I share my bed and my life with. I want a real relationship with you, *bambino*." He didn't think he could spell it out any clearer than that, and she deserved his full honesty after everything he had put her through. Somehow though, even knowing she felt this way too, it was still terrifying to just lay his soul bare out there.

Emma threw herself against him so suddenly it almost winded him and wrapped herself tightly around him like a child would to a parent. She squeezed him as tightly as she could.

"I want that too," she whispered so softly it was barely audible and his heart swelled tenfold, he slid his hand back into her hair, resting her head against him and cradling her close.

"You better not be crying again," he joked, warming more when she tilted back to look up at him with wide happy eyes and the most gorgeous of Emma smiles, the one thing that had always captivated her to him was that genuine smile. Even eons ago when they first met, any hints of her genuine smile had floored him.

"No tears … Brownie's whatsits." Emma attempted some sort of disastrous salute that had him grinning like a kid, pushing her hand down with an indulgent look. She maybe wasn't so perfect at everything she did, but she was perfect enough.

"This … us … it's really happening?" Jake needed to say it aloud, needed to get to grips with the fact this was real, and she wasn't just a dream, resulting from a major emotional breakdown at losing her.

"It looks that way." Emma wiggled her fingers into Jake's and pulled his hand to nestle against his own chest beside her face, he could feel the soft sensation of her breaths on his wrists and it was sending tingles all through him.

"You may need to pinch me a couple of times to believe it, shorty." Jake slid her off of his body so he could bridge the height difference and kiss her once more, his hand freed from hers was now skimming across the softest expanse of creamy throat, across her shoulder slowly. Her skin felt like the softest velvet.

Emma looked suddenly so very serious, her facial expression dropping in an instant and her body tensing as quickly, she looked up at him with wariness.

"What about Marissa?" Her voice broke subtly, emotion under the surface and pain in the depths of those eyes, he cursed internally. Hating that this was one situation he couldn't just wipe away, even for her.

"I don't want her! I didn't want her! It was a stupid drunken mistake. I'll be there for the baby but as far as she's concerned, she means nothing. It's you, it will always be

Jake & Emma

you." It's all he had, the best he could do, knowing that it was something he would need to deal with soon. He traced her eyebrow gently, trying so hard to erase that goddamn soul-crushing look of doubt in her eye. She was thinking about the one thing that could potentially ruin what they hadn't even started yet.

"How do you feel about the baby?" she asked sheepishly, and he knew there was no getting around it at that moment. She wanted to feel secure, and it was his job to make her that way.

"I'd be lying if I said I was happy … I'm not … but I did this, and I need to take responsibility. I hadn't ever thought about having kids, so this is all pretty overwhelming right now." Jake screwed up his face at the thought of that wretched whore Marissa crossing his mind's eye, all smug and repulsive.

"Don't walk away from your child." Emma blinked up at him earnestly, her mind obviously following through to what it was like in her own childhood with a guy who didn't want a kid. Jake leaned in to kiss her again, this time to try to erase some of that self-doubt and heartache almost instinctively. He hated that guy for doing that to his beautiful girl.

"That's not me, Emma … I'm nothing like your father. I won't walk away." He pushed her forehead with his reassuringly. "Can we drop this conversation for now as I have something I'd much rather be doing." Jake grinned, determined to take her mind elsewhere and her body too if she was willing. Enough of the delaying and standing in a dark hall surrounded by strangers; he wanted to take her home and make this thing real.

"Such as?" Emma smiled warily, sudden doubt as to his motives and it only made him want to grin. Always a little unsure and childlike, it was something that had always drawn him to her and made him want to take care of her. She had no clue how vulnerable and naïve she often came across even in full-blown school mistress PA mode.

"Taking my girlfriend home and fucking her brains out. It's long overdue." He grinned, hitting her with a ground moving kiss in a bid to recapture some fire between them, hands sliding around her possessively and pushing her back into the wall to support them both.

Emma kissed him back with equal fervor and passion, her body molding to his and hands sliding up inside between the buttons of his shirt. Bodies igniting with raw lust and on the verge of losing control. He knew there was no stopping them now, he was taking her home as soon as he stopped kissing her and never letting her go again.

About the Author

L.T. Marshall is a Scottish born and bred romance writer with more than the average person's life experience. She has been a torrent of wild things—including singer in a girl band, animal rights activist and charity owner, worked in radio and offered jobs in TV.

A passionate, restless soul, who has always found peace in writing—the only way to calm that fiery spirit. She uses her wit and dark humour to her advantage in her works and has been an avid reader for most of her life.

Her influences vary, but from early life and a teen stint in journalism, she applies logic to most of her plot lines, is a self-confessed research fiend, and likes a lot of psychology behind her characters' actions.

She currently resides in Central Scotland with her two children and fiancé of 13 years, making waves in the book world with her signature "WTF moments" she likes to apply in each story, hints of humour and devastating emotional rollercoaster rides.

A note from the Author

I hope you enjoyed my book, it would mean a great deal to me if you took the time to leave me a review on Amazon or Goodreads—or even both. My reviews are something I regularly, and actively read, and appreciate you taking the time to leave me one. x

L.T. Marshall

Find the Author online

You can find L.T. Marshall across all social media and she regularly interacts with fans on Facebook.

Website: ltmarshall.blog
Facebook: facebook.com/LTMarshallauthor
Twitter: twitter.com/LMarshallAuthor
Instagram: instagram.com/l.t.marshall

Printed in Great Britain
by Amazon